*Cory stole another glance at Wade and wondered at herself.*

If ever a guy looked like a bad risk for even something as simple as friendship, he was it. Yet for some reason she was opening up to him. Not much, but enough that she could get herself into trouble if she didn't watch her step.

She ought to be afraid of him, the way she was afraid of everything else. Instead all she could do was notice how attractive he was.

Wonder if that hard line of his mouth would feel as hard if he kissed her.

What that hard body would feel like against her soft curves.

★★★

Become a fan of Silhouette Romantic Suspense books on Facebook and check us out at www.eHarlequin.com!

D0391926

Dear Reader,

This book was born out of a couple of things—an experience a friend had and my own study of the difficulties involved with the Witness Protection Program. But these were just the germs of the idea.

Cory and Wade's story is much larger and involves a huge measure of healing for them both. Even as Cory is being stalked by a killer, they both have to come to terms with old scars and learn to trust again. When your life has been shattered, and trust ripped away, that's not an easy thing to do.

It doesn't always take much to destroy our sense of security in life, a sense that we must have in order to carry on. But once it's gone, getting it back is a huge task and not everyone does it the same way.

I hope you enjoy the story of two people who fight to regain their lost belief that life can be good.

Hugs,

Rachel Lee

# RACHEL LEE

## A Soldier's Redemption

ROMANTIC
*SUSPENSE*

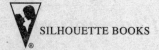

SILHOUETTE BOOKS

Recycling programs
for this product may
not exist in your area.

ISBN-13: 978-0-373-27705-6

A SOLDIER'S REDEMPTION

Copyright © 2010 by Susan Civil Brown

Visit Silhouette Books at www.eHarlequin.com

**Printed in U.S.A.**

**Books by Rachel Lee**

## RACHEL LEE

was hooked on writing by the age of twelve, and practiced her craft as she moved from place to place all over the United States. This *New York Times* bestselling author now resides in Florida and has the joy of writing full-time.

Her bestselling Conard County series (see www.conardcounty.com) has won the hearts of readers worldwide, and it's no wonder, given her own approach to life and love. As she says, "Life is the biggest romantic adventure of all—and if you're open and aware, the most marvelous things are just waiting to be discovered."

For my dad, who taught me that a person is measured by their dedication to honor, duty and loyalty.
You lived those values, Dad. And they live on in me.

# Chapter 1

The knock on the door, as always, caused Corinne Farland's heart to skip a beat. Some lessons, once learned, could never be unlearned.

But after a year in Conard County, she found it a little easier to go to the front of the house. As always, she twitched the curtain aside at the front window by the door and looked out. She recognized Gage Dalton instantly, with his scarred face and his sheriff's uniform. Gage was her main protector these days.

She hurried to disengage the alarm system, then opened the door and smiled, an expression that sometimes still felt awkward on her face. "Hi, Gage."

He smiled back, a crooked expression as the burn scar on one side of his face caused one side of his mouth to hitch oddly. "Hi, Cory. Got a minute?"

"For you, always." She let him in and asked if he'd like some coffee.

"I'm coffeed out," he said, still smiling. "Too many cups of Velma's brew and my stomach starts reminding me I'm mortal." Velma was the dispatcher at the sheriff's office, a woman of indeterminate age who made coffee so strong few people could finish a single cup. The deputies, however, sucked it down by the pot.

She invited him into her small living room, and he perched on the edge of her battered recliner, his tan Stetson in his hands.

"How are things?" he asked.

"Okay." Not entirely true, maybe never truc again, but the bleak desert of her heart and soul were not things she trotted out. Not for anyone.

"Emma mentioned something to me." Emma was his wife, the county librarian, a woman Cory admired and liked. "She said you were a bit tight financially."

Cory felt her cheeks heat. "That wasn't for distribution."

Gage smiled. "Husband-and-wife privilege. It doesn't go any further, okay?"

She tried to smile back and hoped she succeeded. Things were indeed tight. Her salary as a grocery-store clerk had been tight from the beginning, but now because times were hard, they'd asked everyone to take a cut in hours. Her cut had pushed her to the brink, where canned soup often became her only meal of the day.

Gage shook his head. "I'll never in a million years understand how they work this witness protection program."

Cory bit her lip. She didn't like to discuss that part, the part where her husband, a federal prosecutor, had become the target of a drug gang he was going after. The part where a man had burst into her house one night and killed him. The part where the feds had said that for her own protection she had to change her identity and move far away from everything and everyone she knew and loved.

"They do the best they can," she said finally.

"Not enough. It's not enough to buy you a house, give you a few bucks, get you a job and then leave you to manage. Not after what you've been through."

"There was some insurance." Almost gone now, though, and she was clinging to the remains in case of an emergency. She'd already had a few of those with this house they'd given her, and it had eaten into what little she had. "And they did do more for me than most." Like a minor plastic surgery to change her nose, which caused an amazing transformation to her face, and the high-tech alarm system that protected her day and night.

"Well," he said, "I'd like to make a suggestion."

"Yes?"

"A friend of a friend just arrived in town. He's looking for a place to stay awhile that's not a motel, but he's not ready to rent an apartment. Do you think you could consider taking a roomer? You don't have to feed him, just give him your extra bedroom."

She thought about that. There was a bedroom upstairs, untouched and unused. It had a single bed, a dresser and a chair, here when she had moved in. Her own bedroom was downstairs, so she wouldn't have this guy next door to her at all times.

But there were other things, darker fears. "Gage..."

"I know. It's hard to trust after where you've been. But I checked him out. Twenty years in the navy, all documented. Enough medals to paper a wall. You've met Nate Tate, haven't you?"

"Of course." She'd met the former sheriff. He might have retired, but apparently he still made it his job to know everyone in the county. She'd even had dinner with him and his wife a few times at their house. "Of course."

"Well, this guy is a friend of his son's. I don't know if you've met Seth Hardin."

She shook her head.

"Well, that's a story for another day. But Seth is a good sort, and he suggested this guy come here for a while to decompress."

"Decompress?" She didn't know if she liked the sound of that. "I don't know…"

"I'm not asking you to babysit." Gage smiled again. "This guy is quite capable of looking after himself. He just needs some time away. A change of scene. And he's not a talker. I doubt you'll know he's in the house most of the time."

"I'll think about it." But she had to admit, she trusted Gage, and she needed the money.

"How about I bring him inside and introduce you?"

Fear jammed into her throat. Every new person represented risk. Every single one. Hiding had become her raison d'être, and each time she had to meet someone new, the experience resurrected old fears.

"Let me get him," Gage said before she could argue. "He's in my car."

She wanted to scream for him not to do this, but she sat frozen, her fingers instinctively going to her side where the scar from the bullet still sometimes hurt. Where was her will? Her ability to say no? She seemed to have lost that on one dark night a year ago. Ever since, she had moved through her days like an automaton. Doing what was expected, pretending she cared. The truth was that the only thing she ever really felt anymore was fear. And grief. Sometimes fury.

She heard Gage limp back onto the porch, and with him

came a considerably heavier tread. She rose, an instinct these days, not out of courtesy, but out of a need to be able to flee if necessary.

First she saw Gage, but forgot him instantly as she looked at one of the biggest men she had ever seen. He must have been at least five inches over six feet, and even wrapped in a chambray shirt and jeans, he looked to be built out of concrete. Powerful. Strong. Overwhelming.

Scariest of all was the absolute lack of expression on his face. It was a hard face and appeared as if it would yield to nothing at all. His eyes were as black as chips of obsidian, and so was his short hair. She couldn't begin to guess a thing about him, not even his age.

Inside she quailed, helplessly, feeling like a mouse staring down a hawk.

But then he spoke, in a voice as deep as the rumble of thunder. "Ms. Farland. I'm Wade Kendrick." He didn't offer his hand.

The words sounded reluctant. As if he were no happier about putting her out than she was about taking this risk.

And his reluctance somehow eased her fear. "Hi," she said. "Have a seat."

He looked around as if deciding which chair might hold him. He finally took one end of the sofa. Cory sat on the Boston rocker, and Gage eased into the recliner again. The sheriff clearly suffered constant pain, but he never spoke of it.

"Okay," Gage said, since no one else seemed to be willing to talk. "Wade here needs a room indefinitely. Don't know how long, which is why he can't rent an apartment just yet. He's willing to pay monthly for a room. No food."

"I'll eat out," Wade said. "I don't want to get underfoot."

She appreciated that at the same time she wondered at it. He didn't look like a man who gave a damn about such things. "It's not…much of a room," she said hesitantly.

"I don't need much."

Nor did he volunteer much. Of course, she wasn't volunteering anything, either.

"I guess, if you think it's worth it," she finally said. "I've never done this before."

"Ma'am, it's worth it to have a place to lay my head."

She needed the money, and she trusted Gage. Battering down the fear that never entirely left her, not even in her dreams, she said, "Go take a look at the room. It's upstairs. There's a bath up there, too, and it'll be all yours because I have one down here."

The man rose and without another word headed up the stairs at the rear of the living room. Cory glanced at Gage, feeling her heart flutter a little. Panic? Fear? She couldn't tell anymore, since the only feelings she had left were bad ones.

"It'll be all right, Cory," Gage said kindly as they listened to the heavy footsteps overhead. "Sometimes we all need a bolt-hole. That's all he wants."

She could understand that. She was living her entire life in a bolt-hole now.

She stiffened as she heard boots start down the stairway. She didn't want to turn and look, afraid of the impact this huge stranger had on her. But she couldn't evade looking at him for long, because he came to stand in front of her.

"It's just what I need," he said. He pulled out his wallet and handed her six hundred-dollar bills, crisp from the bank. "I'll go get my stuff."

Then he walked out and Cory sat staring at the money in her hand. She was used to seeing money at work, but not holding so much and knowing it was her own. Her hand shook a little.

"That's too much," she almost whispered. It was as much as she made in a month.

Gage shook his head. "He offered it, Cory. It's what he thinks the room is worth."

A minute later, Wade returned carrying a large heavy duffel bag. And that was it. In a matter of less than half an hour, she had gained a roomer, a roomer who carried his entire life, it seemed, in a bag.

How apt was that?


After Gage left, she had to deal with the uneasiness of hearing someone above her head for the first time since she had lived here. She could tell what he was doing by the sounds the rumbled through the floor: unpacking and putting things in the battered dresser.

She needed to give him a key, she realized, and felt her heart lurch at the thought. Her safety not only lay behind a new identity, but also behind locks that were always fastened, and an alarm system the feds had installed. The idea of giving a stranger both a key and the alarm code very nearly caused her a panic attack.

But then she remembered how easily those men had gotten to her and her husband, and knew that no lock or alarm in the world would protect her if she opened her door at the wrong time.

*God,* she thought, *stop this, Cory!* The whole reason she was here in out-of-the-way Conard County, Wyoming, the whole reason she was working as a grocery clerk instead of a teacher, with all the public documents that would require, was so that she *didn't* have to look over her shoulder for the rest of her life.

Nothing about her life now in any way resembled her

life before. Not even her work. Not even her face. That was where her safety lay, not in locks and alarm systems.

She heard Wade come down the stairs. This time she made herself look at him. He hadn't changed, but she felt a shiver of fear anyway. This was still the man Gage had felt safe bringing into her life, and he might be big and appear ready to kill with his bare hands, but Gage trusted him. And she trusted Gage.

"I need to give you a key and show you the alarm code, Mr. Kendrick," she said. Her voice sounded weak, but at least it was steady.

He stood at the foot of the stairs, looking at her. "You comfortable with that?" he asked.

How had he guessed? Was her terror written all over her face? "I…you live here now. You need to be able to come and go when I work."

"No."

"No?" What kind of answer was that?

"I can manage."

She felt a bit stunned by his response. He could manage? He was paying what she considered to be an exorbitant rent to use that lousy bed and bath upstairs for a month, but he was willing to be locked out when she was gone? Had he read her fear so clearly? Or did she stink of it?

Probably the latter, she thought miserably. How would she know? She'd been afraid for so long.

"I'm going out to get sheets, towels, a few other things," he said after a moment. "Which direction should I head?"

Another thought struck her. "Do you have a car?"

"I can walk."

"I could walk, too," she said, feeling a smidgen of her old self spring to life. The resurrection was almost as painful as the death, but at least it was only a small thing, and thus a small pain she could endure. "But if you need a bunch of things, then you might need an extra arm."

"I'll manage."

"Yeah. You'll manage." Sighing, she stood up. "I'll drive you. I need some food anyway." And because of him she now had the money to buy it. Guilt, if nothing else, goaded her.

She went to get her purse. Before they stepped out, however, she insisted on giving him her spare key, and showing him the code for the alarm. If he thought it was odd there was such an advanced alarm system in such a ramshackle house, he didn't indicate it by word or look.

Instead he asked just one question. "Motion detectors?"

"Down here at night. I turn them on separately. Same code. Did you see the keypads upstairs in your bedroom?"

"Yes."

"Well, if you need to come down here at night, you can turn off the entire system from up there, too. To turn off the motion detectors, use the small keypad beside the big one. The rest of the system is on the big pad." She made herself look at him then. Another shiver passed through her as she realized this man could probably snap her in two if he wanted to. Once she had never had those kinds of thoughts. Now she had them all the time. "If you leave, for any reason, and I'm not here or awake, please turn on the entire system."

He nodded. Nothing in his face said he thought that was strange.

She explained the panic buttons, which would direct a call instantly to police, fire or ambulance. Their mere existence reminded her of all that had happened.

And none of it would have done her a damn bit of good fifteen months ago.

Then she set the alarm. It gave them only forty-five seconds to get out the front door and close it. It was long enough.

The U.S. Marshals had also given her a car along with the house. It wasn't a standout that might draw attention. In fact, it was practically a tank, four years old already, guzzling gas in a way that pained her conscience, but her protectors had insisted. The engine was new, as of a year ago, and was a full V-8 with more power than she would ever need.

Because if they came after her, they wouldn't give her a chance to get in a car and get away. She was sure of that. Someday soon, she promised herself, as soon as she could find a way, she would try to trade it in for a smaller but reliable car. She didn't need this steel cocoon.

If she could say nothing else for the Suburban, it gave Wade Kendrick plenty of room. She doubted he could even squeeze into the subcompact she hoped to have someday.

He didn't say another word until she dropped him off in front of the department store. Then it was just, "Thanks."

"When should I pick you up?"

He shrugged. "I won't take long. I'm not picky. Whenever is good for you."

Well, her needs were essentially meager, too. Not even with the extra money could she afford to be reckless. Cooking for one just depressed her, but she made herself buy something more nutritious, like vegetables, and salad fixings, and some chicken. She could shop for more after her next shift, but right now she was off for three days.

Three whole days, and now with a stranger in her house.

Evenings were long here in the summer, the sun not even hitting the horizon until after nine. But as it sank lower in the west, the dry air failed to hold the heat, and the early evening was starting to cool down by the time she emerged from the market with her two cotton bags of groceries. She drove back to the department store, and found Wade already outside on the curb. Apparently he'd bought more than one or two items, to judge by the number of bags, and she was glad she hadn't let him walk. She suspected that if she had, he'd have made several trips because of bulky pillows and blankets as well as sheets and towels.

And he probably wouldn't have said a thing about it. Gage had been seriously guilty of understatement when he said the guy didn't talk much.

She waited while he put his purchases in the back next to her groceries, then he climbed up front beside her.

"Thanks," he said again.

"You're welcome."

And not another sound from him. It was almost as if he were trying to be invisible in every way. Out of sight, out of hearing, out of mind.

If he'd been one of her students, she would have concluded that silence came from secrets, terrible secrets, because nothing about him indicated shyness. But he wasn't a student, he was a grown man, and maybe the same metrics didn't apply.

They reached the house and she pulled into the short driveway and parked. She never used the garage because it provided hiding places over which she had little control.

As soon as she put the car in Park, Wade climbed out. "I'll get your groceries, too," he said.

Part of her wanted to argue that she could manage, but she recognized it for what it was: a desire to exert some control, *any* control, over her life again. The man offered a simple courtesy, and maybe it was his way of expressing his gratitude for the ride. She knew better than to prevent people from offering such little acts of kindness, especially when they had just received one.

Ah, hell, she thought. She didn't ordinarily swear, but this day was beginning to make her want to. Needing to take someone into her sanctuary to pay the bills was bad enough. But finding that the teacher in her still existed, lived and breathed even though it was now forbidden to her, actually hurt.

She felt surprised that it still hurt. After the last year she had thought she was incapable of feeling any lack except the lack of her husband. God, she missed Jim with an ache that would probably never quit.

Head down, she climbed the front porch steps, going through her key ring for the house key. She had keys from the store, keys for the car, a key for the garage…so many keys for such a narrow life.

Just as she twisted the key, she heard the phone ring. It was probably work, she thought, needing her to come in to cover for someone who was sick. Eager for those hours, she left the door open behind her for Wade, punched in the alarm code as fast as she could, and ran for the cordless set in the living room.

She picked it up, punched the talk button, and said, "Hello?" Let it be more than a couple of hours. Make it a couple of days. God, she needed the hours.

A muffled voice said, "I know where you are." Then nothing but a dial tone.

The phone dropped from her hands and her knees gave way.

They'd found her.

## Chapter 2

"What's wrong?"

She looked up from the floor, at the huge man who had entered her life barely two hours ago. He stood in the doorway, his arms full of bags. She tried to breathe, but panic had locked her throat. Speech was impossible, and she couldn't answer that question anyway. Not to a stranger.

Finally she managed to gasp in some air. The instant she recovered her breath, even that little bit, tears started to run. And then she wanted to run. To get in her car and drive as far as she could on what little money she had left, which wouldn't be far at all in that damn Suburban.

And then she realized that if they'd found her, even stepping out her front door could cost her her life.

"Ma'am?"

The giant dropped the bags, and crossed the short

distance between them. He squatted beside her. "Put your head down. All the way down."

Somehow, with hands that seemed too gentle for someone she had already identified as threatening, he eased her down onto the floor, then lifted her legs onto the couch. Treating her for shock, she realized dimly as the wings of panic hammered at her.

"What happened?" he asked again.

The adrenaline had her panting. Who should she call? The Marshals? She knew what they'd do, and God help her, she didn't want to do that again.

"The sheriff. I need to talk to Gage."

At least he didn't question her again. Instead he reached for the phone she had dropped and pressed it into her hand.

"Need me to leave?" he asked. "I'll just go unload the car…"

He shouldn't hear this, but around his dark eyes she saw something like genuine concern. Something that said he'd do whatever was best for her, regardless of what it might be.

Her throat tightened. So few people in her life who would care if she lived or died anymore. Even the Marshals would probably just consider her a statistic on their chart of successes and failures.

"I…" She hesitated, knowing she wasn't supposed to share her true situation with anyone. Not anyone. But what did she have to say that he couldn't hear? She didn't have to mention anything about the witness protection program or her real identity because Gage already knew.

"It's okay," he said. "Just don't get up yet. I'll get the rest of the stuff from the car."

Amazing. He rose and went back to unloading as if she

hadn't just done the weirdest thing in the world: collapse and then demand to call the sheriff.

Amazing.

But she realized she didn't want her car left unattended and unlocked with bags in it. Bags in which someone could put something. And she didn't want her front door open indefinitely, or the alarm off. Her life had become consumed by such concerns.

Muttering a nasty word she almost never used, she brought up Gage's private cell phone on her auto dialer. He answered immediately.

"Cory Farland," she said, aware that her voice trembled.

"Cory? Did something happen?"

"Gage I…I got a phone call. All the guy said was, 'I know where you are.'"

Gage swore softly. "Okay," he said. "Okay. Most likely it was just a prank. You know how kids are when they have time on their hands. Stupid phone calls are the least of it."

"I know, but…"

"I know," he said. "Trust me, I know. I'm not going to ignore it, okay? Stay inside. Don't go out at all, and keep that alarm on. Do you have caller ID?"

"No, I can't afford it."

Another oath, muffled. "I'm going to remedy that as soon as possible. But Cory, try not to get too wound up. It's probably a prank."

Yeah. She knew kids. Probably a prank, like Prince Albert in the can. Yeah. A prank. "Okay."

Gage spoke again. "Think about it, Cory. If they'd really found you, why would they warn you?"

Good question. "You're right." She couldn't quite believe

it, but he was right. She drew another shaky breath, and felt her heart start to slow into a more normal rhythm.

"I'm not dismissing it, Cory," Gage said. "Don't misunderstand me. But I'm ninety-nine-point-nine percent certain it's some kind of prank."

"Of course." She said goodbye and disconnected, then lay staring at her ceiling. It was an old ceiling, and watermarks made strange patterns, some like faces she could almost identify. Like the face of the man who had killed Jim and almost killed her.

She heard the front door close, the lock turn, the sound of the alarm being turned on. The tone pierced what suddenly seemed like too much silence, too much emptiness.

She heard footsteps and turned her head to see Wade. Still impassive, he looked down at her. "How are you feeling?" he asked.

"I'm fine. I'm fine." Life's biggest lie, and it rose automatically to her lips.

"Your color is a bit better. Need help getting up?"

"I can do it, thanks." Yeah, she could do it. Get up, go to the kitchen, put her groceries away and resume the pretense of normalcy. Because there was no other option. All her options had been stolen over a year ago.

Sighing, she pulled her feet off the couch and rolled to her side to get up. A steadying hand was there to grip her elbow, surprising her. She looked into the rigid, unrevealing face of Wade Kendrick and wondered if he were some kind of instinctive caretaker.

She should have protested the touch. But all of a sudden, after a year of avoiding contact with other people, she needed it, even just that little bit of a steadying hand offered out of courtesy.

"Thanks," she said when she was on her feet. "I need to put groceries away."

One corner of his mouth hitched up just the tiniest bit. His version of a smile? "I think," he said slowly, "it might be best if you sit for a bit. I can put your groceries away, and you can supervise."

She should have argued. The independence thing had become of supreme importance to her since circumstances beyond her control had gutted her entire life. But she didn't feel like arguing at all. No, with her knees still feeling rubbery, and perishables like frozen food and milk in her two shopping bags, the task needed to be done soon, and she honestly wasn't sure she could manage it.

Adrenaline jolts had a high price when they wore off. So she led the way into the kitchen, her knees shaking, and sat at the chipped plastic-topped table while he emptied her two bags and then asked where each item went. He went about it with utter efficiency: economy of words and economy of movement both.

And she felt very awkward, unable to engage in conversation. She'd lost most of her conversational ability over the past year because she didn't have a past, at least not one she could talk about, and lying had never come easy. So she had become limited to the most useless of topics: the weather, work, a recent film. No depth or breadth of any kind.

And when faced by a man like this, one who seemed disinclined to talk, all she could do was sit in her chair and squirm.

"There," he said when the last item was put away. Then he faced her. "If you're okay now, I'll take my stuff upstairs."

She should have said thank-you and left it at that. That's what she *should* have done. But all of a sudden, maybe because of the phone call, being alone was the last thing she wanted. Solitude had been her fortress for a long time, so why she should want to breach the walls now, she couldn't understand. But she did anyway.

"If I make coffee," she said, "would you like some?"

One eyebrow seemed to lift, but she couldn't be quite sure. This was a man who seemed to have lost use of his face. Either that, or he had trained himself to reveal absolutely nothing. And the question about coffee seemed to give him pause. He treated it as if it needed real consideration.

"That would be nice," he finally said.

Only then did she realize she was almost holding her breath. Maybe she feared rejection of some kind. How could she possibly consider a *no* over a cup of coffee to be rejection? God, was she beginning to lose her mind?

It was, of course, entirely possible. In the past year she'd come perilously close to living in solitary confinement with only her memories.

"Okay." She tried a smile and it seemed to work, because he nodded.

"I'll just take my stuff up and be back down in a minute," he said.

She watched him walk out of the room and noticed his broad shoulders and narrow hips. The ease with which he moved in his body, like an athlete. Yes, she was definitely slipping a cog somewhere. She hadn't noticed a man that way in a long time, hadn't felt the sexual siren song of masculinity, except with Jim, and since Jim not at all.

She didn't need or want to feel it now.

Shaking her head, she rose and found that her strength seemed to have returned. Making the coffee was an easy, automatic task, one that kept her hands busy while her mind raced.

Surely Gage had been right. The killers wouldn't warn her they were coming. So it *must* have been kids pulling a prank. When she thought about it, her own reaction to the call disappointed her. There'd been a time when she would have reached the same conclusion as Gage without needing to consult anyone at all. A time when she hadn't been a frightened mouse who couldn't think things through for herself.

She needed to get that woman back if she was to survive, because much more of what she'd gone through the past year would kill her as surely as a bullet.

Piece by piece, she felt her personality disassembling. Piece by piece she was turning into a shadow of the woman she had once been. She might as well have lopped off parts of her own brain and personality.

How long would she let this continue? Because if it went on much longer, she'd be nothing but a robot, an empty husk of a human being. Somehow, somewhere inside her, she had to find purpose again. And a way to connect with the world.

As one of the Marshals had said when she argued she didn't want to do this, "How many people in this world would give just about anything to have a chance to start completely fresh?"

At the time the comment had seemed a little heartless, but as it echoed inside her head right now, she knew he'd had a point. She hadn't liked it then, didn't like it now, but there was a certain truth in it.

A fresh start. No real reason to fear. Not anymore. If they were going to find her, certainly they'd have done so long since.

Wade returned to the kitchen just as the drip coffeemaker finished its task. "How do you like it?" she asked.

"Black as night."

She carried the carafe to the table, along with two mugs and filled them, then set the pot on a pad in the center of the table. She always liked a touch of milk in hers, one of the things she hadn't had to give up in this transition. She could still eat the foods she preferred, drink her coffee with a little milk, and enjoy the same kinds of movies and books.

Maybe it was time to start thinking about what she hadn't lost, rather than all she had.

Brave words.

She sat across the table from Wade, trying not to look at him because she didn't want to make him feel like a bug under a microscope. But time and again her gaze tracked toward him, and each time she found him staring at her.

Finally she had to ask. "Is something wrong? You keep staring at me."

"You're a puzzle."

She blinked, surprised. "You don't even know me."

"Probably part of what makes you a puzzle," he said easily enough. His deep voice, which had earlier sounded like thunder, now struck her as black velvet, dark and rich.

"Only part?" she asked, even though she sensed she might be getting into dangerous territory here.

"Well, there is another part."

"Which is?"

He set his mug down. "It seems odd to find a woman so terrified in a place like this."

She gasped and drew back. His gaze never left her face, and he didn't wait for a denial or even any response at all.

"I know terror," he continued. "I've seen it, smelled it, tasted it. You reek of it."

She felt her jaw drop, but she couldn't think of one damn thing to say, because he was right. *Right.*

"Sorry," he said after a moment. "I suppose I have no business saying things like that."

Damn straight, she thought, wishing she'd never asked him if he wanted coffee. Wishing she'd never agreed to share a house with him. Those dark eyes of his saw too much. Way too much.

He'd stripped her bare. Anger rose in her and she glared at him. How dare he? But then, hadn't she all but asked for it?

He looked down at his mug, giving her a break from his stare, from his acute perception.

She thought about getting up and walking into her bedroom and locking the door. Hiding, always hiding. The thought stiffened her somehow, and instead of fleeing she held her ground. "Is it that obvious?"

He shook his head. "Probably not to anyone who hasn't been where I've been. Except for when you got that call, you put on a pretty good act."

"My entire *life* is an act," she heard herself snap.

He nodded, and when he looked at her again something in his gaze tugged at her, something that reached toward her and tried to pull her in. She looked quickly away. None of that. She didn't dare risk that.

"Look," he said finally, "I don't mean to upset you. I just want you to know…" He trailed off.

She waited, but when he didn't continue, she finally prodded him. "Want me to know what?"

"I'm not useless. Far from it. So if…if you need help, well, I'm here." Then he poured a little more coffee in his mug and rose, carrying the mug away with him.

She listened to him climb the creaky stairs and wondered what the hell had just happened.

Wade made up his bed with the skill of long years of practice in the navy. Perfectly square corners, the blanket tight enough to bounce a quarter off. His drawers were just as neat, everything was folded to fit a locker though, so the items didn't exactly match the drawers, but the stacks were square.

Old habits die hard, and six months of retirement hadn't killed any of them.

He sat on the wood chair in the corner of the room, and focused his mind like a searchlight on the present, because looking back got him nowhere, and the future seemed impossible to conceive.

That woman downstairs was as scared as any green combat troop he'd ever seen. As scared as the women and kids he'd seen in situations he didn't want to remember.

He hadn't expected to find that here. Hadn't bargained on the feelings it would resurrect. He'd come to this damn county in the middle of nowhere because Seth Hardin had promised he'd find peace and solitude, and that everything here was as far from his past as he could possibly get.

Right.

Apparently Seth hadn't known about this woman. Corinne Farland. Cory. Regardless, who the hell would have thought that he'd find this mess through the simple act of renting a room?

He leaned over and lifted the coffee mug from the top of the dresser, draining half of it in one gulp. Good coffee.

The back of his neck prickled a little as he thought about the situation, and he never ignored it when the back of his neck prickled. That sensation had saved his skin more than once, or someone else's skin.

But he couldn't figure out why the hell Gage Dalton had brought him to this particular woman. There must be other rooms for rent in this county. Surely.

Well, maybe not. The place didn't exactly look huge. So it *could* just have been coincidence. But he didn't believe much in coincidence. At some level, conscious or otherwise, Gage had thought of this woman, her terror and her room.

And there was a reason for that, a reason that made the skin on the back of his neck crawl. Cory's level of fear suggested a long-term, ongoing threat.

And here he was, smack in the middle of a place he thought he'd left behind. A place he *wanted* to leave behind.

He needed to normalize, to stop being a SEAL and start being a reasonably ordinary member of society again. He needed to stop sleeping with one eye always open, constantly ready for death to lunge out of any shadow or hole. He needed to let his reflexes slow again, at least to the point where someone wouldn't risk death simply by trying to wake him from sleep, or by moving too fast in the corner of his eye. That's what he needed, and that had just skittered out the door of his immediate future.

Because downstairs there was one hell of a scared woman, and she shouldn't feel that way. And a phone call, a simple phone call, had caused her to collapse.

From what he'd seen of Conard County and Conard City so far, he would have called the place bucolic.

Well, that was a hell of a reaction for a bucolic place.

It wasn't normal. It didn't fit.

Apparently he would have to keep sleeping with one eye open.

He could leave, of course, but that didn't even truly appear on his menu of options. He couldn't walk away from her terror.

Someone that terrified needed protecting.

For a change, he decided, he'd like to provide the protection, rather than the terror.

A bitter smile twisted his mouth. That, at least, would be a change. A much-needed change.

And wasn't that what he'd come here for?

The phone didn't ring again, thank God. Cory ate a small salad for dinner, then tried to settle in with the TV. She didn't think she could focus on one of the library books stacked on the small table beside the rocking chair, because her mind seemed to have turned into a flea, insisting on hopping from one thing to another, all totally unrelated. Even the sharpness of fear didn't seem able to get her full attention.

So it was easier to turn the TV on, for the noise, for the visual distraction, for the occasional moments in which she could actually tune into the program, whatever it was.

She noted that her roomer upstairs had grown quiet, utterly quiet. Probably sleeping, but with her senses on high alert, the inability to guess what he was about made her uneasy. Solitude was her friend, her fortress, her constant companion.

But she'd invited in an invader, and his silence was worse than the noise he'd made while settling in.

She flipped quickly to the weather station, but too late, because the image of a crime-scene team entering a home where a man lay dead, just a reenactment, was enough to set off a string of memories she tried never to visit.

Jim lying there, bleeding from multiple wounds. Trying to crawl to him despite the wound in her own side, gasping his name, knowing somehow as she crawled that he was lost to her forever.

She squeezed her eyes shut as if that could erase the images that sprang to mind. Gentle, determined Jim, a man with a huge smile, a huge heart and a belief in making the world a better place. A man who could talk to her with such kindness and understanding, then in a courtroom or deposition turn into a circling shark, coming in for the kill.

A gifted man. An admirable man.

The man she had loved with every cell of her being.

Their last dinner together. Jim had taken her to one of the best restaurants in Tampa to celebrate a positive pregnancy test that very morning. They'd laughed, coming up with silly names they would never in a million years give their child.

And shortly after midnight, everything that mattered in her life vanished. At least she didn't mourn the pregnancy as much as she might if she had had time to get accustomed to the idea. That little mark on the stick had scarcely been real to her yet when the gunshot ended it all.

But Jim...Jim had been everything. Jim and her students. The life they had barely begun to build together after only two years.

Now she drew a shaky breath, trying to steady herself, trying to prevent the gasping sobs she had managed to avoid for months now.

But awake, or asleep, she still heard the banging on the door. Banging that had sounded like the police. Jim had laughed drowsily as he climbed from bed to answer it.

"Somebody probably just tried to steal my car," he had said. His car was also a joke between them, a beater he'd gotten in law school. It was certainly not worthy of stealing, but the very expensive stereo he'd put in it was.

She had heard him open the door then...

Her mind balked. Her eyes snapped open. No, she couldn't do this to herself again. No way. It was done, the nightmares permanently engraved on her heart and mind, but that didn't mean she had to let them surface.

Sometimes she even scolded herself for it, because while

grief was natural, and the fear she felt equally so, every time she indulged herself in grief or fear, she knew she was giving that man even more power over her than he had already stolen from her.

And he had already stolen everything that mattered.

The phone rang, jarring her. This time she didn't jump for it, this time she didn't think it was work calling. Part of her wanted to let it ring unanswered, but she didn't even have an answering machine, and what if it was Gage?

Slowly, reluctantly, she reached for it, coiling as tight as a spring. So tight some of her nerves actually objected.

"Hello?"

"Cory, it's Gage. I just wanted you to know a few other women have reported similar calls, so it was probably just a prank, okay?"

Her breath escaped her lungs in a gasp of relief. "Thanks," she said. "Thanks."

"And I'm getting caller ID put on your service. The phone company says you should have it within a few days. And don't worry about the cost. The department will pay for it."

"Oh, Gage…" Words deserted her yet again. Of all the places on this earth the Marshals could have put her, she was grateful they had put her in a town with Gage Dalton.

"Hey," he said kindly. "We take care of our own around here. It's not a problem."

Before she could thank him again, he was gone.

"Is everything all right?"

Startled, she nearly cried out, and turned to see Wade Kendrick at the foot of the stairs. How had he come down so silently? Earlier his tread had been heavy. Or maybe she'd just been so distracted. She drew a few deep breaths, trying to steady her pulse.

"I'm sorry," he said quietly. "I didn't mean to startle you. I heard the phone ring, and after the way you reacted earlier..."

"Of course. Of course." She closed her eyes and consciously tried to relax, at least a bit. It didn't happen easily anymore, that whole relaxing thing. "Everything's okay. Gage...called." But what could she tell him about the call? Even a few words might be too much.

He waited, and it was clear to her that he wasn't satisfied. But he didn't ask, he just waited. And somehow his willingness to wait reassured her. She couldn't even understand it herself.

"I got a nasty phone call earlier," she said slowly.

He nodded. "I didn't think it was a funny one."

"No." Of course not. And now she was sounding like an idiot, she supposed. She gathered herself, trying to organize her words carefully. "Gage just wanted me to know that several other women received similar calls."

One of his eyebrows lifted. "Really."

"Probably just kids."

"Maybe."

His response didn't seem to make sense. "Maybe?"

"Well, that would depend, wouldn't it?"

"On what?"

"On what has you so scared, and who else received the calls."

"What in the world do you mean?"

He shrugged. "Life has made me suspicious."

"Oh." She bit her lower lip, realizing that nothing in her life had prepared her for dealing with a man like this. He seemed to come at things from a unique direction, unlike anything she was familiar with.

He started to turn away. "Well, as long as you're okay..."

He didn't ask a single question. She found that intriguing, given what little he had figured out about her in the short time since he moved in. Any other person would have been asking dozens of question, but this man just seemed to accept that she was afraid, she must have good reason for it and that it was none of his business.

In that moment she thought it possible that she might come to like him.

"Wade?"

He stopped and turned back to her. He didn't say a word, simply looked at her.

"I, uh…" How could she say that she didn't want to be alone? That she was tired of being locked in the prison of her own thoughts? That even though solitude had provided her only safety for a year now, she was sick of it, and sick of her own company. Tired enough of it all to feel an impulse toward risk. Just a small risk.

"Should I make coffee?" he asked.

He had understood, though how she couldn't imagine. She might have been about to ask him anything, tell him anything.

All she said was, "Thanks." Because there was nothing else she *could* say.

She switched the TV off so she could listen to his movements in the kitchen. Everything he needed was beside the drip coffeemaker, so he wouldn't have trouble finding it. And finally she could afford to have more than one cup each day. Imagine that, being reduced to one cup of coffee and a can of soup each day.

Sure, there were plenty of people in the world who had less, but her life had never before been restricted in such a way. She'd always been luckier than that. Always. Until recently.

Wade returned finally with two mugs, hers with exactly the right milkiness. The man missed nothing. Nothing.

He sat across from her on the easy chair, sipping his own coffee, watchful but silent. Maybe this wasn't going to work at all. How did you converse with a block of stone? But she needed something, anything, to break the cycle of her own thoughts.

Man, she didn't even know how to start a conversation anymore! Once it had come as naturally as breathing to her, but now, after a year of guarding every word that issued from her mouth, she had lost the ability it seemed.

Wade sipped his coffee again. He, at least, seemed comfortable with silence. After a couple of awkward minutes, however, he surprised her by speaking.

"Do you know Seth Hardin?"

She shook her head. "I know his father, but I've never met Seth."

"He's a great guy. I worked with him a lot over the years. He's the one who recommended I come here."

Positively voluble all of a sudden. "Why?"

He gave a small shrug. "He thought it would be peaceful for me."

At that a laugh escaped her, almost hysterical, and she broke it off sharply. "Sorry. Then you walk into this, a crazy widow who collapses over a prank phone call. Some peace."

His obsidian eyes regarded her steadily, but not judgmentally. "Fear like yours doesn't happen without a good reason."

It could have been a question, but clearly it was not. This man wouldn't push her in any way. Not even one so obvious and natural. She sought for a way to continue. "Gage said you were in the navy."

He nodded. "For more than half my life."

"Wow." She couldn't think of anything else to say.

"Yeah." Short, brief. After another moment he stirred. "You need to talk."

She tensed immediately. Was he trying to get her to explain? But then he spoke again, easing her concern.

"I'm not a talker." Another small shrug. "Never was. Making conversation is one of the many things I'm not good at."

"Me, either, anymore. I wasn't always that way."

He nodded. "Some things in life make it harder. I'm not sure I ever had the gift."

"Maybe it's not a gift," she said impulsively. "Maybe most of what we say is pointless, just background noise."

"Maybe. Or maybe it's how we start making connections. I stopped making them a long time ago."

"Why?"

He looked down into his mug, and she waited while he decided what he wanted to say, and probably what he didn't.

"Connections," he said finally, "can have a high price."

Man, didn't she *know* that. Maybe that was part of the reason she'd kept so much to herself over the past year, not simply because she was afraid of saying the wrong thing. Maybe it was because she feared caring ever again.

"I can understand that," she agreed, her lips feeling oddly numb. As if she were falling away again, from now into memory. But her memory had become a Pandora's box, and she struggled to cling to the moment. To now.

The phone rang again. She jumped and stared at it. Gage had already called. Work? Maybe. Maybe not.

Wade spoke. "Want me to answer it?"

A kind offer, but one that wouldn't help her deal with reality. She'd been protected almost into nonexistence, she realized. Protected and frightened. At some point she had to start living again, not just existing.

So she reached for the phone, even as her heart hammered and her hand shook. "Hello?"

"Cory!" A familiar woman's voice filled her ear. "It's Marsha." Marsha from work, a woman she occasionally spent a little time with because they had some similarities, some points of connection they could talk about. But they'd never really gotten to the point of random, friendly phone calls.

"Hi, Marsha. What's up?" Her heart slowed, her hand steadied.

"I got a phone call. I think Jack has found me!"

Cory drew a sharp breath. While she hadn't shared her story with Marsha, she'd learned a lot of Marsha's story over the past year. "What makes you think that?"

"The person said he knew where I was!"

"Oh. Marsha, I got one of those calls, too. Did you report it to the sheriff?"

"A phone call like that?" Marsha laughed, but there was an edge to it. "Why would he even listen to me?"

"Because I got one of those calls. And a few other women did, too."

Marsha fell silent. Then hopefully, "Others got the same call?"

"Gage thinks it was a prank. I reported it and so did some others."

In the silence on the line, Cory could hear Marsha start calming herself. She waited patiently until she could no longer hear Marsha's rapid breathing. Then she asked, "Do you want to come over?" She'd never asked that before, even though she'd gone to Marsha's a few times. Explaining expensive alarm systems could get…messy, and involve lying.

"No. No. I guess not. If Gage thinks it's a prank, and I'm not the only one to get a call, I must be okay."

"So it would seem."

"But I'm going to get a dog," Marsha said with sudden determination. "Tomorrow, I'm getting a dog. A big one that barks." Then she gave a tinny laugh.

"If it helps you to feel safer."

"It'll help. And if I'm this nervous after all this time, I guess I need the help. Want to do coffee in the morning?"

That meant going out, and Gage had told her not to. But that had been before he decided the calls were a prank. Cory hesitated, then said, "Let me call you about that in the morning."

"Okay. Maybe you can help me pick out a dog."

As if she knew anything about dogs. "I'll call around nine, okay?"

"Okay. Thanks, Cory. I feel a lot better now."

When Cory hung up, she found Wade sipping his coffee, quietly attentive. After a moment's hesitation, she decided to explain.

"My friend Marsha. She got one of those calls, too."

"Why did it frighten her?"

"Her ex was abusive. Very abusive. She's afraid he might find her."

He nodded slowly. "So she's hiding here, too?"

"Too?" She didn't want to think about what his use of that word meant, how much he must have figured out about her.

He said nothing, just took another sip of coffee. Then, at last, "What did the caller say?"

"Just 'I know where you are.'"

Another nod. "That would be scary to someone who doesn't want to be found."

And she'd just revealed a whole hell of a lot. She ought to panic, but somehow the panic wouldn't come. Maybe because having listened to Marsha, some steely chord in her had been plucked, one long forgotten. Prank call or not, at least two women were going to have trouble sleeping tonight, and that made her mad.

"Why would some idiot do this?" she demanded. "I don't care if it was kids. This isn't funny. Not at all."

"I agree."

His agreement, far from settling her, pushed her into a rare contrarian mood. She knew kids, after all, had taught them for years. "They don't think," she said. "They probably got the idea from some movie and are having a grand old time laughing that they might have scared someone."

"Maybe."

"They wouldn't realize that some people might really have something to fear."

"Maybe."

She looked at him in frustration. "Can you manage more than a few syllables?"

At that he almost smiled. She could see the crack in his stone facade. "Occasionally," he said. "How many syllables do you want?"

"Just tell me why you keep saying *maybe*."

"I told you, I'm suspicious by nature. Tell me more about your friend Marsha."

"Why? What? I told you her story, basically."

He set his cup on the end table and leaned toward her, resting his elbows on his knees and clasping his hands. "Try this. Have you both always lived here or did you move here? Are you about the same age? Any similarities in appearance?"

Just as she started to think he had gone over some kind

of edge, something else struck her. For a few seconds she couldn't find breath to speak, and when she did it was a mere whisper. "You think someone could be trying to find one of us?"

"I don't know." The words came out bluntly. "A sample of two hardly proves anything. But I'm still curious. Will you tell me?"

She hesitated, then finally nodded. "Marsha and I are sort of friends because we…share a few things. We both moved here within a couple of weeks of each other, almost a year ago. We work together at the grocery."

"Your ages? And your appearance?"

"We don't look like twins."

"I didn't think you did. But otherwise?"

"I think we're as different as night and day." Indeed they were. Marsha had short red hair, a square chin, green eyes and a bust a lot of women would have paid a fortune for. Cory, on the other hand, now had chin-length auburn hair—which she hated because she had to keep it colored herself to hide her natural dark blond—and brown eyes that had looked good when she was blonde but now seemed to vanish compared to her hair. The Marshals had given her a slight nose job, though, replacing her button nose with something a little longer and straighter. They hadn't messed with her bust, though. That was still average.

"Are those differences that could be easily manipulated?"

She didn't like where he was going with this, didn't like it at all. "You *are* suspicious." But then, so was she. All of a sudden Gage's phone call seemed a lot less reassuring. "Marsha and I don't look at all alike." But how sure was she of that?

"Then I'm overly suspicious." He leaned back, picking up his coffee again. "Way too much so."

"Why?"

"Because I've lived my life in the shadows. Suspicion is part of my creed. I never take anything at face value." He shrugged. "Best to ignore me, I suppose."

It might have been except for her past. Had she an ordinary life behind her, it would have been easy to dismiss him as a nut. But she couldn't quite do that.

"Why," she asked finally, "would he call so many? If someone was after either of us, a whole bunch of phone calls wouldn't make sense, would it?"

He shrugged. "Like I said, just ignore me."

Easier said than done, especially when he seemed to have been following some train of thought of his own. But he said nothing more, and she really couldn't imagine any reason he should be suspicious.

But of one thing she was reasonably certain: the man who would want her dead wouldn't need to call a bunch of women to scare them. In fact, it would be the last thing he would do. Because calling her would warn her, and if she got scared enough to call the Marshals, they'd move her.

Even though moving her would take time, it would certainly make killing her more difficult while she was under constant surveillance once again, as she had been in the three months between the shooting and her eventual relocation.

So it had to be a prank. Surely. She clung to that like a straw in a hurricane.

Because it was all she could do.

# Chapter 3

In the morning, Cory decided to go for coffee with Marsha after all. She had a little money to spare because of Wade, and a cup of coffee at Maude's didn't cost that much, especially if she avoided the fancier drinks that Maude had begun to introduce, taking her cue from the major coffee chains. So far Cory didn't think there was a huge market for "mocha decaf lattes" here, even though she loved lattes herself, but they were now available if anyone wanted them.

Marsha expressed huge gratitude for the call. In her voice, Cory heard a stress that matched her own. She hadn't slept well at all last night, tossing and turning, one nightmare following another.

When she finally gave up trying to sleep, it was only five-thirty in the morning. She'd grabbed a book from the table beside her bed and had attempted to read for a couple of hours. In the end, though, the words might as well have been random letters, none of the story penetrated, and she thought she might have dozed a bit.

Wade must still be asleep, she thought when at last she reset the house alarm and slipped out the door. She'd been the only one to change the alarm settings since she awoke—she'd have heard the tone if anyone had—and she hadn't heard him moving around.

Nothing strange in that, she supposed, except she had somehow expected him to be an early riser. Why? Because he'd been in the navy? Not everyone in the navy worked days and slept nights. She knew that much. Maybe he'd had some kind of night duty. Which got her to wondering what kind of work he'd done, and how he'd gotten enough medals to paper a wall, according to Gage.

Well, she could always try asking him, but she doubted he would answer. And how could she complain about that when she kept her own secrets?

It was a lovely summer morning, and she could have walked to Maude's but uneasiness made her take the Suburban anyway. Besides, she told herself, trying to pretend she wasn't acting only out of over-heightened fear, if Marsha really did want to get a big dog, the Suburban might be the best way to get it home.

Marsha was already there at a table with coffee in front of her. Hardly had Cory slid into a seat facing her when Maude stomped by, slamming a mug down and filling it. A little bowl of creamer cups already sat in the middle of the table.

Cory actually felt a smile twitch at the corners of her mouth. In a year she'd never bought anything here except coffee, and Maude had apparently given up on talking her into anything else. Once in a blue moon, a piece of pie would be slapped down in front of her but never show up on the bill. Interesting woman, Maude. Cory was quite sure she had *never* met anyone like her.

Marsha smiled at her, but the expression didn't reach her eyes. She looked exhausted, and Cory suspected they had both spent nights filled with nightmares and restlessness.

"I'm glad that you told me a bunch of women got the same call," Marsha said.

"I don't know how many, but Gage indicated there were a few of us. That's why he thinks it's a prank."

"Makes sense." Marsha opened another little cup of half-and-half and lightened her coffee even more. "And I guess if a few reported the calls, there were probably more like me who never called him at all."

"Probably," Cory agreed. "You look like you slept about as well as I did."

Marsha's laugh was short and hollow. "Yeah, we look like a pair of zombies, don't we? I just couldn't stop thinking about Jack all night, about all the things he threatened to do to me. But it's been almost a year, so he probably never wanted to come after me. He just wanted to scare me."

And Marsha had plenty of reason to be scared, considering the things her ex had done to her. Cory wanted to say something reassuring, but couldn't. How could she reassure anyone when she was living with a similar terror herself? Her pursuers might have more reason to try to track her, since she could help identify one of them as a murderer, but did that mean Marsha's ex was necessarily less determined?

"Are you still going to get a dog?"

Marsha nodded. "I called the vet before I came here. He says he has a couple of dogs I might like and that they're naturally protective breeds."

"That sounds good."

"I told him I wanted a big dog, but he recommended against it."

"Really?"

Marsha gave a small, tired laugh. "He asked me how much I wanted to walk it, and did I want to be able to hold it in my lap..." Her voice broke, then steadied. "Sorry. I'm just tired. But anyway, the idea of a dog that would curl up on my lap sounded good, and with the hours we work, I couldn't walk a dog at the same time of day every day..." She trailed off, sighed and looked down into her coffee.

All of a sudden, Cory felt something she hadn't felt in far too long: a desire to protect someone besides herself. The urge rose fiercely, and burned away some of the fear.

Those men had stolen her life, but for the last year she'd let them steal *her,* too. She'd let them turn her into a quivering, frightened recluse whose only concern was surviving each day.

How much more twisted could she get? How could she let them keep doing this to her? She wasn't the only person on this planet with fears and needs. Look at Marsha. What had she ever done except marry the wrong man? Yet, she, too, had been driven into a hole in the ground.

Angry, Cory couldn't sit still another moment. She slapped some bills on the table, to cover both their coffees, and stood. "Let's go get your dog. You need a reason to smile."

Marsha appeared startled, but then began to grin. "Yeah," she said. "Let's go get that dog."

"Cute and cuddly," Cory said. "The cutest, cuddliest one we can find."

Because there still had to be something good in life, and a dog was as good a start as anything else.

\* \* \*

Conard County wasn't a heavily populated place, so it had a limited tax base and had to cut some corners. Hence the vet and animal control shared property and kennels, and the vet, Dr. Mike Windwalker, was on retainer to care for the impounded animals. Like most small-town vets, he handled everything from horses to the occasional reptile.

A handsome man in his mid-thirties, he'd replaced the former vet five years ago and seemed to enjoy his broad-spectrum practice. He had one assistant, though he could probably have used more.

"You picked a good day to do this," he remarked as he led Marsha and Cory back through his office toward the kennels. "I'm not very busy so I'll have time to help you make a good match."

As they approached the wire gate beyond which lay the sheltered kennels, the sounds of dogs barking started to build.

"They know we're coming," the vet said with a smile. "But before we go in…" He turned to Marsha. "I want to know a bit more about why you want a dog. Just for protection? Or would you like a companion? And can you afford much dog food?"

Marsha bit her lip, then admitted, "I'm tired of being alone so much. Yes, I want a dog that can alert me when someone comes, but I think I'd like to have one to love, too. And play with. I'd love to play with a dog. As for food—" she wrinkled her nose "—I probably shouldn't have a dog with a huge appetite."

At that Mike Windwalker smiled. "Then I have a couple of good ones for you. Love and protection can come in small sizes as well as large."

Cory stayed back a bit, watching as Mike introduced Marsha to various small dogs. She didn't want to get too interested in the process because when Wade left, unless she got a better job or more hours at her current one, she simply wouldn't be able to take care of a pet. Nor, when she thought about it, could she have one running around at night with the motion detectors on.

But it was so hard to resist all the puppy-dog eyes. It would have been entirely too easy to choose one for herself, and she had to remind herself again and again that she couldn't afford it.

But she felt a definite stab of envy when Marsha eventually settled on a Pomeranian. "Definitely loyal," the vet said approvingly. "She'll let you know any time anyone approaches the house and these dogs can be relied on to fight for their owners if necessary." He shook his head. "People often underestimate the protectiveness of the small breeds. There are ways to get around a dog, any dog, but these small guys have hearts like lions."

Marsha definitely looked as if she'd fallen in love. And while she naturally had a cheerful nature, it was often eclipsed behind spurts of worry. Right now, she looked as if she didn't have a worry in the world.

"Just one caveat," the vet said. "I offer obedience classes for free, and with this one you'd be wise to take them."

"I will."

"I'm starting a new class Saturday morning at nine."

Marsha beamed at him. "I'll be there."

When she drove back home a short while later, Cory felt she'd managed to accomplish at least one good deed, small as it was. And it *had* been small. She hadn't been able to give Marsha the dog, or even help her decide which one was best, but she suspected Martha might not have acted so quickly on her own, simply because living in fear had a way of paralyzing you. Even small decisions sometimes seemed too big to make.

And that had to stop, she told herself sternly. It had to stop now. For too long now she'd been little more than a wasted lump of human flesh.

Wade must have heard her pull up, because he was waiting for her at the foot of the stairs. Apparently he'd been sleeping because his hair had that tousled look, and his blue sport shirt hung open over his jeans.

Cory couldn't help herself. She stopped dead and stared. That was some chest, smoothly muscled, bronzed and just begging for a touch. Oh, man, as if she needed this now.

With effort she dragged her gaze upward and then wished she hadn't, because she saw in his obsidian eyes that he hadn't missed her look. He revealed nothing about his reaction to it, though, nor did he make any attempt to button his shirt.

"Did Marsha get her dog?" he asked before the silence got long enough that she wouldn't be able to pretend he hadn't noticed what she'd been noticing.

"Yes. A Pomeranian."

"I had a buddy who had one. He called it his pocket piranha."

The remark was utterly unexpected, and it bypassed every short circuit the past year had put in Cory's brain. She giggled. Actually giggled.

A faint smile leavened Wade's face. "He liked to bite my ankles."

That seemed even funnier. "Such a stupid dog," she giggled again.

"Stupid?"

"Taking on someone your size? That's stupid."

Wade's smile widened just a hair more. "He knew I wouldn't hurt him. Dogs have good instincts."

She laughed again, still amused by the image. Then it

struck her that he seemed to have been waiting for her. "Is there something you need?"

"Well, actually…" He hesitated. "I know the deal was I would eat out. But I was wondering, would you mind if I bought groceries and cooked for myself? I'll leave things squared away so you won't even notice I was in there."

For some reason she liked the idea that he wouldn't be leaving her alone three times a day to hunt up a meal. Amazing how far she had come in less than a day. What had initially seemed like a threat now seemed like a bulwark. Nor was this a matter she wanted to take issue over.

"I don't mind." Although she was a little surprised that he'd felt it necessary to say she wouldn't even know he'd been in the kitchen. Most people wouldn't have bothered to mention it, unless asked.

She drew a sharp breath, and all of a sudden her heart tugged. She'd heard promises like that before, unsolicited ones. *You'll never notice I was in there.*

A few faces floated before her eyes, youngsters all, former students all. And she knew what phrases like that really meant. Could this big, powerful man with all his medals still carry scars like that? After all this time?

But she couldn't ask.

"Is something wrong?"

His question shook her back to the moment. "No. Really. My mind just wanders sometimes. I think I spend too much time alone." Her laugh this time carried no mirth, but was more of an apology.

"I'll just go get some groceries then."

She shook her head. "It may go against your grain to look for help, but you shouldn't try to carry groceries home when I can drive you. Just let me get a glass of water, and then I'll take you."

For an instant she thought he would argue. Something about him said that he didn't relinquish autonomy easily, or accept help easily, at least not from virtual strangers. But then he nodded. "Take your time. Obviously I'm in no rush."

Wow, she thought as she headed toward the kitchen, at this rate they might even start to converse in whole paragraphs. She took her time drinking her water because she heard him climb the stairs again, probably to brush his hair, button his shirt and pull on some shoes.

Sure enough, five minutes later she heard him descend again. She finished her water and went out to the foyer. "Ready?" she asked, though it was clear that he was. His boots had given way to some comfortable and battered deck shoes, and he'd buttoned and brushed.

"If you are," he replied.

She grabbed her purse and keys, saying, "Let's go then."

"You're sure you don't mind?"

There it was again, a niggle. A hint. She looked at him, wishing she could just come right out and ask. But that might be a mistake, because he'd probably just get angry at her prying, and rightfully so. He hadn't poked into her life, so she should give him the same respect.

"I don't mind at all," she assured him, and summoned a smile. Aware now of what might lurk in his past, she felt old lessons rising up to guide her. And the thought that she might, through her training, help this man feel a bit more comfortable made her feel better than she had in a long time. She might not be able to teach anymore, but it would be so good to *help*.

Always assuming, of course, that she wasn't totally wrong about him.

The drive to the store was silent, but she was getting

used to that with him, and didn't feel as uncomfortable as she had just yesterday.

When she pulled into a parking slot, though, he spoke. "You don't have to wait for me," he said. "If there's something you need to do."

She shook her head. "Not a thing. Maybe I'll check and see if they can give me any extra hours."

She climbed out and locked the car. Another car pulled in nearby, and the driver, a man, appeared to be fussing through some papers. Probably lost his shopping list, Cory thought with a small sense of amusement.

Wade waited for her, then walked beside her across the parking lot, measuring his stride to hers.

"You work here?" he asked.

"Yes." Then she volunteered, "We all had our hours cut back a couple of weeks ago."

"That hurts. No wonder you need a roomer. How's Marsha managing?"

"Somewhat better. She gets an alimony check."

He paused just after they stepped through the automatic doors and looked at her. "Then her ex knows where she is."

"Theoretically not. The court sends the checks and is supposed to keep her address private."

He nodded. "Good thing."

She headed for the manager's office at the customer service desk while he got a cart and started down the aisles. Interesting that he'd expressed concern for Marsha, she thought. Apparently a real heart beat behind the stone.

The manager, Betsy Sorens, greeted her with her usual wide smile. "Sorry, Cory. No extra hours. Not yet anyway. You're at the top of my list though when we can start adding them."

Cory felt almost embarrassed. "Why should I be at the

top of the list? That doesn't seem right, Betsy. So many others need hours, too."

"We all need hours, some more than the rest. You're self-supporting. A lot of the other employees have other sources of income."

Cory felt her cheeks color a bit. "Still…"

Betsy shook her head. "You're a good employee. If I can do a little something for you, I will."

A customer came then with a complaint, so Cory smiled, waved and left. Wandering around the store with nothing to buy and nothing to do felt odd. Almost without thinking, she paused occasionally to straighten the stock on the shelves.

She hated to have time hanging on her hands, and she'd certainly had too much of that in the past year. She'd once been busy almost every second of the day, between Jim and her job. Now she had endless hours of free time, and that meant too many hours to think.

Hours to think about the past, about that phone call yesterday, hours to let her fear and anxiety build when there was no real reason for it. Certainly they would have found her by now if they were going to.

She met Wade in one of the aisles and glanced into his cart. There wasn't much there yet.

"Having trouble?" she asked.

One corner of his mouth lifted. "You might say that."

"What's wrong?"

"I've been mostly eating in mess halls or eating out of boxes for years. I know the basics about cooking, but shopping for one person isn't as easy as I thought."

That was a whole lot of syllables, she thought, and for some reason that made her smile. "I have an idea."

"What's that?"

"I hate cooking just for myself. Why don't we take turns cooking for each other?" she suggested.

"Are you sure? You could be taking an awful gamble."

"On your cooking?"

"What else would I mean?" he asked.

"I'm willing to take it. And if it doesn't work out, well, I could teach you to cook. Or you could just let me do it."

He shook his head. "No way am I going to let you cook for me every night. That wasn't part of the deal."

She could almost see him closing down again, as if the idea that he might lean on her concerned him. "Okay then, cooking lessons if you need them."

That seemed to satisfy him. Armed with the idea that they'd take turns cooking seemed to loosen him up though. He started tossing more items into the cart.

"I should go buy some more groceries," she said suddenly. "I just realized, I only bought enough for myself for a couple of days."

"Let me," he said. "It'll cover the cooking lessons I'll probably need."

She opened her mouth to argue, but then shut it. This man absolutely *needed* to feel as if he wasn't a burden. That much was clear to her so she endured it as he spent money on foods she would have ignored because of the price.

But the thought of cooking some of the dishes she had once *loved* to cook and eat soon had her thinking of ingredients she should buy.

"I don't know what's needed to cook some of this stuff," Wade said. "Grab whatever you need." It was enough to get her going.

Along the way she saw the man from the parking lot again. He was pushing a cart and carrying a piece of paper, and nodded when he saw her. She managed to smile back. Evidently he'd found his list.

Before they even reached the checkout, two more people had smiled and nodded at her. She was used to that when she was working and in uniform, but for the first time it struck her that folks around here might be friendly as a matter of course. Maybe she ought to make a bigger effort.

By the time they left the store with another four bags of groceries, she was looking forward to dinner.

And how long had it been since she'd last felt that way? No, she wasn't going there, not when she was actually feeling good, feeling almost *normal,* for the first time in a year. There was absolutely nothing wrong with feeling good, she reminded herself. Nothing at all. Jim wouldn't have wanted her to become the woman she had been during the past year.

The shadow that hovered over all her days tried to return when she had to deal with the alarm, but she refused to let it. No more of that, she told herself, as if something as simple as a command to herself could change her entire outlook and banish the fear that never quite deserted her.

But at least she was making an effort, and when she looked over the past day, she felt glad those kids had made that stupid call. Yes, it had thrown her into a tizzy, and yes, it had upset Marsha just as much, but in the course of reacting to it, she had helped Marsha a little bit. Now she could at least help Wade learn to cook.

Little things, but more purposeful than almost anything since that awful night. Time to cherish her tiny victories.

"When do you usually like to eat dinner?" she asked as they worked together to put things away. She stopped a moment to look at her refrigerator. It hadn't been that full while she lived here, ever. And now it held an embarrassment of riches.

He paused, a box of cornstarch in hand, and looked at her. "Ma'am, you're talking to a SEAL. I learned to eat when the food was there."

"Oh." She bit her lip. "A SEAL? Really?"

"Really."

That would explain at least some of it, she thought, how he could look so hard and dangerous at times. It might even explain his lack of expression and his disinclination to talk. Hesitantly she said, "I can't imagine what it must have been like."

"No."

And that closed the subject. Well, it would if she let it. How much did she want to risk now that they'd found some common ground? But the silence seemed heavy in some way, no longer comfortable. With one word he'd fixed an image of himself in her mind and she didn't know how to absorb it. Nor did she know why she wanted to cross the barrier he had set so firmly in place with that one word.

Recklessly, she didn't take the warning. "I've seen programs about SEALs," she offered.

"A lot of people have." He started folding her cotton grocery bags neatly.

"The training looks terribly hard."

"It is."

Volumes of information. She almost sighed. "I saw another program about an operation where the SEALs had to board a ship at sea to remove a container of plutonium that could have been used to make a bomb."

"Yes."

"It's amazing what you guys can do."

"Most people have no idea what we do." With that he put

the folded bags in a neat stack on her counter and walked from the kitchen.

She listened to him climb the stairs, listened to the creak as he went into his room.

And with him departed the little bit of positive purpose she'd found just today.

# *Chapter 4*

Cory felt bad. For the first time in forever, she had felt positive, felt ready to reach out, however tentatively. And she'd blown it.

She had pressed Wade, even when her instincts had warned her that might be a mistake. Apparently her skills had atrophied over the past year. There'd been a time when she would have handled that approach a whole lot better.

Or would she? How could she even know anymore? For so long she'd been curled inward in a tight ball around her own fear and pain. Maybe she would have flubbed the conversational attempt even back then. Wade, after all, was a grown man, not one of her kids. His barriers had to be even higher, even more deeply ingrained.

Regardless, she wished she'd just kept her mouth shut, because it had been surprisingly nice to do ordinary, routine tasks *with* someone else, even a someone she didn't know, and could barely talk with. Just the rhythm of it had probably been one of the most soothing experiences she could remember in a while.

Worse, she was brooding about what surely had to be the most minor of trespasses. It wasn't as if she'd demanded personal war stories or anything. Far from it.

*Let it go,* she told herself. Good advice except that perhaps the worst change in her over the past year was the way she could seldom just dismiss things. Like that phone call last night.

In her previous life, she wouldn't have given it a second thought. Once upon a time, even if it had disturbed her, she'd have been able to shake it off in relatively short order.

Events had changed her. Worry had burrowed mole holes in her mind, ever ready to grant easy access to the next concern that showed up. The stupidest things could run in circles for hours or days, and she could no longer shake them.

But today, thanks to Marsha and then Wade, she'd managed to put that call out of her mind. To put it in its proper place.

But it was still there, ready to pounce the instant she allowed it to. If she sat here too much longer brooding, the fear would steal back in and soon she'd be like a dog gnawing at a bone, unable to let it go.

Finally she stood up, deciding the best thing in the world would be to take a walk. She'd spent too many hours hiding in this house over the past year, and that had turned her into an even worse mess.

She wondered if she had failed to heal because fear had taken over to a paralyzing degree. Which was more ridiculous when she considered the entire weight of the federal government had thrown itself behind making her disappear.

Yes, she was still grieving, but somehow grief and fear had become so intertwined she no longer knew which was which. The one was a healthy thing, the other not.

Today she seemed to have taken two successful baby steps in the right direction. It was time, she decided, to step back out into the sunlight, to start living again the way most other people lived: without the constant expectation of the terrible happening.

Nobody got a guarantee, after all.

Grabbing her keys, leaving her purse behind, she slipped into her jogging shoes then turned off the alarm. She had to turn it off, because once it was set and had been on more than forty seconds, opening and closing the door without triggering the alarm sequence became impossible. Failure to turn off the alarm within forty seconds meant that the police would be called.

So she punched in the code to turn it off, listening to the near-squeal it made. As soon as it was disarmed, she could reset it and safely leave.

But she didn't get to the rearming part.

"Where are you going?"

She turned and saw Wade at the top of the stairs. A spark of annoyance flared, a welcome change from the steady diet of fear she'd been living with. "Out. What business is it of yours?"

"None." His shirt was unbuttoned again, but he still wore his jeans and deck shoes. This time she noticed more than the broad expanse of his chest. She noted his flat belly, the fact that he had the coveted "six-pack" of abdominal ripples, though not overdeveloped. She had to drag her gaze away, back to his face. He started down the stairs. "I'll go with you."

Her jaw dropped a little, and her annoyance grew. "Why? I'm just going to walk around the block."

"I'd like a walk."

But he didn't have to take it *with* her. She almost said so, quite sharply, and then realized something. Her fear hadn't just dissipated on its own today. No, *he* had driven it back.

Now what? Would she insist she go on the walk alone? When she might well get scared again halfway around the block? Was she going to take the offered crutch?

She ought to say no, for her own good. It was high time she started conquering her fears. But then remembering how she had felt when she'd made him leave the room earlier, she decided she didn't want to needlessly offend him again.

It was as good an excuse as any, she supposed, because now that she actually thought about it, she wasn't sure she yet had the courage to take that walk alone. Especially after that phone call last night.

"Damn!" she swore.

He was now at the foot of the stairs, buttoning his shirt, and looked at her. "What?"

"I'm so confused I can't stand it."

"About what?"

She hesitated.

"You don't have to tell me. Walking helps quite a bit."

Giving her emotional space, but not physical space. She looked at him, and for the first time got past the sheer impact of his solidity and strength to notice that he was a handsome man. Very handsome, in a rugged, healthy way.

She sighed. *Not now. Please.* But it was a simple fact that the frisson he made her feel was not fear for her life, but fear of dangerous sexual attraction. With a man as closed off as Wade Kendrick, there could only be pain on that path.

But she was still young enough and healthy enough to feel those urges. Well, maybe that was a good thing. Another part of her coming back to life.

"Are we taking that walk?"

"Uh, yeah." She punched in the codes again and together they stepped out onto the small porch. She set out purposefully in the direction of the town park, thinking it would do her some good to see kids at play again. Among the many things she had avoided in the past year was children, because they reminded her of things lost. But she might be ready to let them remind her of some of the goodness in life.

Once again he measured his pace to hers, as if it came automatically. And once again, he said nothing.

The summer afternoon was warm, the sun as brilliant as it could get this far north. And without warning she found herself talking, although she had to catch herself frequently so she didn't reveal too much.

"I used to live in...down south. Almost in the tropics, actually. I notice the difference in the sun here."

"It is different," he agreed.

"The days are longer in the summer, but the sun never gets as high or bright. And the winter nights are so long here."

"Yeah."

"But at least I don't burn as easily." She managed a small laugh. "In the summer down there you can get a tan walking across a parking lot."

It was his turn to give a small laugh, as if he, too, were trying. "I've been in all kinds of climates."

Well, that was a positive step, she thought. "I imagine so." She was careful not to question. Instead she chose to talk a little more about herself. "I've had a lot to adjust to, and I haven't been doing a very good job of it."

For a few paces he didn't say anything. Then, "I guess it's harder to adjust when you're afraid."

"It's that obvious, huh?"

"Like I said, only to someone who would know fear."

"I don't know whether that's a compliment or a criticism."

"Neither. Just an observation."

"Do you ever get afraid?" As soon as the words were out she realized she might have trespassed too far again, but it was too late to snatch them back. She almost held her breath, wondering if he would turn and walk away.

Instead, he astonished her by answering. "I'm human."

Sideways, but still an answer. She relaxed a bit and looked around, taking in the old trees that lined the street, their leaves rustling ceaselessly in the summer breeze. Nobody else seemed to be out and about, but that wasn't unusual. Here, as everywhere, most couples both needed to work.

"In the evenings," she remarked, "there will often be people sitting out on their front porches. Different from where I used to live. Most of the neighborhoods around me back home were built relatively recently, when it was important to have a privacy-fenced backyard. You'd almost never see anyone out front unless they were doing yard work."

"In most places in the world where I've been, a house is where you sleep or shelter from the elements. The rest of life happens in common areas, on the street, in front of the house. Not for everyone, of course. There are always some who want to keep the unwashed masses away. And in some cultures an enclosed courtyard is considered necessary, but given that several generations of a family live together, it's not exactly isolation."

That was practically half an encyclopedia coming from this man. "Do you think we're losing something with those fenced backyards?"

"Depends on what you want out of life. But once you build that fence, if you're having a barbecue you're not going to have a neighbor who might drop over for a chat and bring a six-pack, and wind up staying on for dinner."

"True." She turned that around for a few seconds. "I don't really know how different it *feels* to live in a place like this," she finally admitted. "Basically, when I come home from work I pass all these probably very nice people on their front porches and go inside and lock myself in."

"Maybe you have good reason."

Maybe she did. Or maybe she'd been acting like a wounded animal that wanted to be left alone in its burrow. The whole point of the Marshals moving her here had been so that she didn't *have* to live this way. Another sigh escaped her.

"I thought," she said reluctantly, "that I was breaking out of the cycle earlier today. I even told myself to go take a walk."

"But?"

"But then I realized that I'd just been distracted. That despite everything, I'm still worried at some level because of that call last night. Oh, I can't even explain it to myself."

They reached the park and found a bench not far from the sidewalk. Nobody else was there, so Cory's hope for distraction was disappointed.

Wade let the silence flow around them with the breeze for a few minutes before he spoke again. "Sometimes," he said quietly, "we get confused because we're changing."

That made her look at him, and for an instant she wished she hadn't because she felt again that unexpected, unwanted attraction. What was going on with her? Why did she suddenly have the worst urge to put her head on the shoulder of a stranger? To feel his arms close around her?

She jumped up from the bench and headed home. Walking it off seemed like the only sane course available to her. "We need to start dinner," she said, the sole explanation she could offer for her behavior. Because there was no way she could tell him that the feelings he awakened in her were nearly as frightening as that phone call had been.

Despite her sudden takeoff, he fell in step beside her before she had made two full strides. Glued to her side. Part of her wanted to resent that, and part of her was grateful for it. Confusion? She had it in spades. At least her fear and grief had been clear, so very clear. No questions there.

Now the questions were surfacing, the conflicting feelings, all the stuff she'd avoided for so long. She forced herself to slow her pace to an easier walk. She'd been running again, she realized. Had she forgotten every other mode of existence?

"Darn," she said under her breath. All of a sudden it was as if someone had held up a mirror, and painful or not she had to look at herself. She wasn't seeing a whole lot that she liked, either.

"Something wrong?" Wade asked mildly.

She stopped midstride and looked at him. Mistake, because the truth burst out of her and she wasn't sure she wanted it to. What did she know about this guy after all? "Has something ever made you stop and take a good look at yourself?"

"Yes."

"What if you don't like what you see?" She didn't wait for an answer, just started walking again. She didn't expect an answer, frankly. It wasn't the kind of question anyone else could answer.

But he surprised her. "You make up your mind to change."

"Easier said than done."

"Always."

Some inner tension uncoiled just a bit. Change? Why not? After all, she'd allowed herself to be changed by life, had just rolled along like a victim. That did not make her feel proud. "Sometimes," she said more to herself than him, "you just have to grab the rudder." She hadn't done that at all since the shooting. Not at all.

"Grabbing the rudder is easier to do when the seas aren't stormy."

She glanced at him again. Oh, there was a story there, and she wished she knew what it was, but she didn't dare ask. This man could disappear even in plain sight, and she didn't want him to disappear again. At least not yet.

For some reason the invader had ceased to be an invader. Maybe just his presence had reminded her that she still had a life to live. Maybe his obvious protectiveness had made her feel just a little safer. Or maybe the attraction she felt was overcoming all the walls she'd slammed into place.

Because she *had* slammed those walls into place. She hadn't built them brick by brick. No, she'd put up the steel barricades almost instantly in the aftermath. Huge parts of her had simply withdrawn from life, no longer willing to take even small risks, like making a friend.

She stole another glance at Wade and wondered at herself. If ever a guy looked like a bad risk for even something as simple as friendship, he was it. Yet for some reason she was opening up to him. Not much, but enough that she could get herself into trouble if she didn't watch her step.

She ought to be afraid of him, the way she was afraid of everything else. Instead all she could do was notice how attractive he was. Wonder if that hard line of his mouth would feel as hard if he kissed her. What that hard body would feel like against her soft curves.

Ah, she was losing her mind. For real. It had finally snapped. After a year of inability to feel anything but grief and anguish, she had finally broken. Now she was looking at a virtual stranger as a sex object.

*Way to go, Cory.* Very sensible. Clearly she couldn't trust herself at all anymore.

Two cars came down the street toward them as they rounded the corner right before her house. She lifted her hand to wave, deciding it was about time to make a friendly gesture. The woman in the first car smiled and waved back. The man in the second car didn't even glance at them.

They reached the door and went inside, resetting the alarm. Without a word, he followed her into the kitchen, evidently ready to get his first cooking lesson. She started pulling things out, preparing to make a dish with Italian sausage and pasta and fresh vegetables. The recipe was one that had emerged one day from a scramble through the cupboards and the realization that the only way she could put together dinner was the stone-soup method.

"I can't trust myself anymore," she muttered, at first unaware that she was thinking out loud. When you lived alone long enough, having conversations with yourself often moved from the mind to the mouth. "Everything's been so screwed up for so long. But then how do I know my thinking wasn't screwed up before? I was living in some kind of enchanted universe before. A place where bad things didn't happen."

She turned from pulling a package of frozen Italian sausage from the freezer and saw Wade standing there, arms folded, watching. And that's when she realized her muttering hadn't been private. Her cheeks heated a bit. "Sorry, sometimes I talk to myself. Bad habit."

"Don't mind me."

"Well, you don't want to hear it. And I'm not sure I want anyone else to hear the mess that's going on inside my head."

"I can go upstairs if you like."

She shook her head. "Stay. I promised to teach you some cooking, and this is a great dish to start with." She passed him the package of frozen sausage. "Microwave, hit the defrost button twice, please."

He took the sausage and did as she asked. Soon the familiar hum filled the kitchen. Green peppers and tomatoes were next, a true luxury these days, washed in the sink and readied for cubing. "Do you like onions?"

"Very much."

So she pulled one out of the metal hanging basket and peeled it swiftly before setting it beside the other vegetables. As soon as she reached for the chef's knife, though, Wade stepped forward. "I can slice and dice. How do you want it?"

"Pieces about one-inch square." She passed him the knife and as their hands brushed she felt the warmth of his skin. All of a sudden she had to close her eyes, had to batter down the almost forgotten pleasure of skin on skin. Such a simple, innocent touch, and it reminded her of one of the forms of human contact she absolutely missed most: touch. Even simple touches. She almost never let anyone get that close anymore, certainly not a man.

A flood tide of forgotten yearnings pierced her, and she drew a sharp breath.

"What's wrong?"

He was so near she felt his breath on her cheek. Warm

and clean. A shiver rippled through her as she fought the unwanted feelings, and forced her eyes open, ready to deny anything and everything.

But the instant her gaze met his, she knew she could deny nothing. His obsidian eyes darkened even more, and she heard him inhale deeply as he recognized the storm inside her. There was a clatter as the knife fell to the counter, and the next thing she knew she was wrapped in his powerful arms.

He lifted her right off the floor and set her on the counter, moving in between her legs until she could feel his heat in places that had been too cold and too empty for so long. This was not a man who hesitated, nor one who finessed the moment.

He swooped in like a hawk and claimed her mouth as if it were rightfully his. An instant later she learned that thin mouth could be both soft and demanding. That his hard chest felt every bit as hard as it looked, and felt even better as it crushed her breasts. His arms were tight and steely, and she should have been afraid of their power, afraid of what he could do to her whether she wanted it or not.

But all she could feel was the singing in her body as it responded to needs more primal than any she had ever imagined. Somehow the dissenting, cautious voices in her head fell silent. Somehow she lifted her arms and wrapped them around his neck, holding on for dear life.

Because this was life. Here and now. Like Sleeping Beauty awakening from a nightmare, she discovered she could want something besides freedom from terror and pain, and that good things were still to be had despite all.

Her body responded to life's call as her mind no longer seemed able to. His tongue passed the first gate of her teeth, finding hers in a rhythm as strong as her heartbeat, a thrusting that echoed like a shout in a canyon until it reached all the way to her very core and came back to her in a powerful throbbing.

A gasp escaped her between one kiss and the next. Her legs lifted, trying to wrap around his narrow hips, trying to bring her center right up against his hardness, trying to find an answer to the ache that overpowered her. Any brain she had left gave way before the demands of her body for more and deeper touches. Her physical being leaped the barriers that had existed only in her mind.

He moved against her, mimicking the ultimate act, not enough to satisfy, but enough to promise. She wanted every bit of that promise. Every bit.

He drew a ragged breath as he released her mouth, but he didn't leave her. No, he trailed those lips across her cheek, down the side of her throat, making her shiver with even more longing, causing her to make a small cry and arch against him. One of her hands slipped upward, finding the back of his head, pressing him closer yet. She wanted to take this journey as never before.

Then the microwave dinged.

All of a sudden, reality returned with a crash. He pulled away just a couple of inches and looked at her, his eyes darker than night. She stared back, hardly aware that she was panting, suddenly and acutely aware of how she had exposed herself.

As if he read her awareness on her face, he stepped back a little farther. The absence of pressure between her thighs made her ache even more, made some part of her want to cry out in loss. But with the return of awareness came a bit of sense.

He didn't pull completely away, as if he knew how sensitive this could become. How dangerous for her, and maybe for him.

Instead, even as she let her legs fall away, he reached out to gently brush her hair with his hand.

"You're enchanting," he said huskily.

Enchanting? No one had ever called her that. She remained mute, unable to speak, knowing that her eyes, her face, her breathing must be telling a truth she didn't want to hear herself say. Not yet, maybe never.

"I forgot myself."

He wasn't the only one. She didn't know what to say, could only stare at him, torn between yearning, loss and the returning shreds of common sense.

He leaned forward, giving her the lightest of kisses on her lips. "I think," he said, "that I'd better cut those vegetables."

She managed a nod, awhirl with so many conflicting feelings she doubted she could ever sort them out. He turned to pick up the knife, and moved down the counter about a foot to the cutting board and vegetables.

"You don't have to be afraid of me," he said, his voice still a little thick. "I'll behave."

Another odd choice of words. As she fought her way back from the frustration of awakened, unmet desires, she tucked that away for future consideration. Right now, the thing she most needed was some equilibrium. Thinking could come later.

Wade, just about to start slicing the vegetables, put the knife down and turned toward her. He gripped her around the waist and set her back on her feet. "Sorry," he said. "Should have thought of that."

She could have slid off the counter on her own, but hadn't because she still felt so shaky. Unable to tell him that, she mumbled her thanks and turned desperately in another direction, away from him, seeking something to keep busy with. This was a simple meal, and he was about to do the major part of the work.

Finally she measured out the penne into a bowl, then walked around him to get the sausage from the microwave. Just act as if it never happened, she told herself. Maybe it never had.

But her traitorous body said otherwise. Oh, it had happened all right, and she suspected the internal earth-quakes had just begun. Even the light brush of her own clothing over her skin, especially between her legs, reminded her that something primal had awakened.

She coated the bottom of a frying pan with olive oil, then began to slowly cook and brown the sausage on medium heat. Her hands still shook a little when she pulled out the stockpot she used for cooking pasta. A cheap pot, it wouldn't have served well for anything that wasn't mostly liquid, and she found herself pausing, suddenly locked in the most ridiculous memory of her previous pasta cooker, an expensive pot with a built-in colander and a smaller insert for steaming vegetables.

It was an odd memory, coming out of nowhere. She had long since ceased to care about the things she had lost during her transition to this new life, but for no reason she could almost feel the weight of that pot in her hands and with it the tearing edge of memories, ordinary memories, the simple kinds of things that should hold no threat whatever. It wasn't a memory of Jim, of their life together. It was just a memory of a damn pot, one she had bought long before she married Jim. Nothing but a memory from the life of a woman who had once slowly built up a kitchen full of all the best cooking utensils because she loved to cook, and part of that expression was using the best of everything.

On a teacher's salary, many of those items had truly

been an indulgence. She had scrimped to buy them, until she had had a kitchen that would have pleased a world-class chef.

And now she was using a five-dollar aluminum stockpot and a chef's knife she'd bought on sale at the grocery store.

How odd, she thought, looking at the pot. How very odd what had once seemed important to her. And how little she usually missed those things now that they were gone. In fact, even had she been able to afford them, she doubted she would have replaced them.

They didn't matter any longer. Who had that woman been, anyway? Had she ever known? She certainly didn't know who she was now.

A faint sigh escaped her, and she put the pot in the sink to fill it with water. Indulgences. Her past life had been full of them, her new life was empty of them. In the midst of the storm, all she could say about it was that she had never known who she was? Had no idea who she had become?

When she started to lift the heavy pot full of water, Wade stepped in and lifted it for her. "Don't call me a pig," he said. "I've just been trained to act a certain way."

She arched a brow at him. "So a woman can't lift anything heavy?"

"Why should she when I'm standing right here?"

Once again she was left wondering how to take him. But this time she asked, emboldened, perhaps, by the fact that he had called her enchanting. "What exactly do you mean? That I'm too weak to do it?"

He shook his head. "No."

That awful answer again, the one that told her nothing. "Then what?" she insisted, refusing to let him get away with it.

He put the pot on the stove. "Would it make you feel better if we had an argument?"

That yanked her up short and hard. Was that what she was doing? Trying to get angry so she could forget the other things he made her feel? Or was this some kind of insistence on independence that actually made no sense? She bit her lip.

He faced her again. "It's my training. It's my background. Call it a simple courtesy."

And he'd done it even though he'd expected her to object. In fact, he'd tried to deflect the objection before it occurred. Would she have even thought he was being chauvinistic if he had not shot that defense out there to begin with?

"You're a very difficult man to understand," she said finally. "Not that you try to make it any easier."

"No. I don't."

"Thank you for lifting the pot."

"You're welcome."

Feeling a bit stiff and awkward now, she returned to cooking. Maybe she should never have agreed to this whole cooking thing. Maybe she should have kept him at a distance, as a roomer she hardly saw.

Because right now she felt too much confusion for comfort.

Confusion and fear. Great companions.

## Chapter 5

Wade went to ground for the night. He had no problem staying out of the way upstairs until sometime in the morning. He had a finely honed instinct that warned him when it was time to become part of the background. Wallpaper. Just another tree in a forest. Now was such a time.

The hours ticked by as he read a novel he'd bought during his bus trip but had never really started. He had plenty to think about anyway as the hours slipped toward dawn. The past he still needed to deal with, the future he needed to create out of whole cloth and finally because he could avoid it no longer, a woman who slept downstairs.

Not quite two days ago, he'd met Cory Farland for the first time. There had been no mistaking that she lived in a constant state of fear, though he didn't know why. Now, in an extremely short space of time, she had made several attempts to break out of that fear, to become proactive, to take charge of even little things. And she had come perilously close to having sex with a total stranger.

He recognized the signs of someone emerging from a terrible emotional trauma. Her actions were a little off center, her reactions misaligned. He didn't even have to try to imagine the kind of confusion she must be experiencing within herself because he'd lived through it.

He wanted to kick himself, though, for giving in to the sexual desire that had been so plainly written on her face in the kitchen. Yeah, she was a helluva sexy woman, but she wasn't a one-night-stand kind of woman. If he'd pursued the matter any further, he might have given her another wound to add to the seemingly heavy scars she already carried.

His own actions had taken him by surprise, though. He usually had much better self-control, and he couldn't imagine why she'd gone to his head so fast. Yeah, it had been a long time, but that was a poor excuse. He'd quit enjoying pointless sexual encounters many years ago. Lots of women were eager to hop into bed with a SEAL, and there'd been a time when he had been glad to oblige.

Not anymore. Not for a long time now. The hero worship, the sense that he was another notch on a belt, had palled ages ago. Nor did he have the least desire for notches of his own.

What he wanted was a connection. And he knew he couldn't make them. As he'd already told Cory, he didn't make them at all. Couldn't afford them, sure. But couldn't make them, either. And he'd long since given up trying to pretend he could. Best to just hold the world at a distance.

But trying to hold the world at a distance didn't mean he could ignore that fact that Cory might need his protection. She seemed afraid in a way that suggested the threat, whatever it was, still lurked somewhere, that she had found no resolution.

It also fascinated him that while she had shared Marsha's story of an abusive husband, she had shared nothing at all about why that phone call had terrified her so. Secrets meant something. And in this case, since her first call had been to the sheriff, he doubted she was on the run from a legal problem.

Which left…what?

And then something clicked together in his brain.

He sat up a little straighter as the circumstances he had so far observed came into focus. Moved here about a year ago, deliberately censored her speech when she spoke about where she came from. Her silences were more revealing than her speech. No offered comparison of her situation to Marsha's. High-tech alarm system when she had little money. And terrible, terrible fear. Collapsing because some anonymous person had said, "I know where you are."

WITSEC. Witness Protection.

He knew the protocols, had been part of WITSEC teams abroad. Usually the protected person was in some kind of trouble up to his neck, and was being protected because he'd agreed to inform against his own cohort.

But he'd bet his jump wings that this woman had never done anything more illegal in her life than speed on the highway. Which meant she had been an innocent witness to a crime and her life was in danger because of it. A crime that had yet to be solved. Nothing else would put her in the protection program. And nothing else would have caused the Marshals to spend so much money on that alarm system. Your average confessing criminal didn't get that kind of care.

He swore under his breath and stared at the closed door

of his bedroom. Every instinct and every bit of his training rushed back to front and center.

No wonder that call had terrified her. No wonder she seemed as jumpy as a cat on a hot stove. No wonder she hadn't been able to create a life for herself here.

Then he remembered something from their walk home that afternoon, and gave himself a huge mental kick in the butt.

Without a thought, he jumped to his feet, dressed in his darkest clothes and his favorite boots. Then he switched off the motion sensors, wishing there was some way to silence the squeal, and headed downstairs. Six months of trying to be normal vanished in an instant.

He barely reached the foot of the stairs before Cory came staggering from her bedroom, her eyes heavy-lidded with sleep, a blue terry-cloth robe held tightly around her with her arms.

"Sorry," he said. "I just needed to move around." *Check the perimeter.* "I didn't think it would do much good for your sleep if I clomped around upstairs."

Her brown eyes regarded him groggily. "What time is it?" she asked finally, smothering a yawn.

He glanced at the highly complex dive chronometer on his arm. He hadn't worn it in months, but for some reason he'd put it on during the night. As if something had niggled at him, saying it was time to go on duty. "A little past five," he answered.

"Good enough time to start the coffee," she said, yawning again.

"I can do it. Why don't you go back to bed?"

"I'm one of those people. Once I'm awake…" She gave a shrug and shuffled toward the kitchen.

"I'm just going to walk around the block," he said.

"Fine." She didn't even look back, just waved a hand.

So he turned off the alarm and turned it back on again so he could slip out the door. He was going to hate that alarm before long. It hampered him. He should have been able to do this without waking her at all.

On the other hand, he was glad he didn't have to leave her unprotected in there. Outside the sun was rising already, casting a rosy light over the world. He walked around the house, then set out to jog around the block.

He should have noticed it sooner, but the guy who had parked beside them at the store, then met them in the aisle had been the very same man who had driven past them on Cory's street in a *different car.* Evidently he'd relaxed more over the past six months than he'd realized, because he *never* would have failed to notice that immediately when he was on the job. Now that he'd made the connection, he had to know if they were still being watched. Had to make up for lost time.

But neither the mystery man nor either of his cars showed up.

Which of course meant nothing except that if the guy was indeed shadowing Cory, his prey was in for the night. Reaching the house again, his breath hardly quickened by his fast jog over such a short distance, he stepped inside once more, tended the squealing, annoying alarm and made his way to the kitchen.

Cory sat at the table, chin in her hands, eyes half-closed as she waited for the coffeemaker to finish.

"Do you ever hate that alarm?" he asked as he pulled mugs out of the cupboard and put one of them in front of her.

"Sometimes." She gave him a wan smile. "I never love it, that's a fact."

"I'll get used to it," he said as he reached for the coffee

carafe and filled both their mugs. Then he got the half gallon of milk out of the fridge for her and placed it beside the carafe on the table.

"Thank you. You do get used to it."

"Sorry I woke you," he said again. "But I just couldn't sit still another moment." Not exactly as simple as that, but just as true.

"No need to apologize. I may not get back to sleep now, but I usually can manage a nap in the afternoon if I need it. I'll be fine." She poured maybe half a teaspoon of milk into her coffee, then raised the mug to her lips and breathed the aroma in through her nose. "Fresh coffee is one of the greatest smells in the world."

"It is," he agreed. He pulled out the chair across from her, but looked at her before he sat. "Do you mind?"

Something crossed her face, some hint of concern, but it was gone fast and he couldn't make out what it meant. She waved toward the chair. "Help yourself."

He turned the chair so he could straddle it, then sat facing her. "Looks like it's going to be a nice day out there."

"Probably. I miss the rain, though."

"Rain?"

She covered her mouth, stifling another yawn. "Back in…back where I used to live, this time of year we'd be having afternoon thunderstorms almost every day. I miss them."

"But you get some here, too, right?"

"Sometimes. Not nearly every day, though. In a way, they're prettier here."

"How so?"

"You can see so far you can almost watch them build out of nothing. Sometimes anyway." She gave a little shake of her head. "No trees to get in the way if you drive out of town."

"True."

"But there's not as much lightning with them. I used to love the lightning shows in—" Again a sharp break. An impatient sound. "We used to watch them some nights. One storm in particular, there must have been a lightning bolt every second or so. And when they'd hit the ground, you could see a green glow spread out from them and rise into the sky. I only saw it in that one storm, but I was fascinated enough to research it."

"What was it?"

"Corona discharge. It's actually quite common in electrical discharges, but often we don't even see it. The air around gets ionized as the charge dissipates. Most corona discharges aren't dangerous, but when lightning is involved, it can be."

She sipped her coffee, then held the cup in both hands with her elbows on the table. "You must have seen storms all over the world."

"I have. Monsoons, hurricanes, typhoons and then just the regular buggers, which can be bad enough."

"Yes, they can. There's so much power in a thunderstorm. Incredible power. I used to te—" Another break. She looked down, effectively hiding her face behind her mug.

Teach? he wondered. Deliberately, he let it pass. The last thing he wanted to do was cause her fear because she'd revealed something she felt she shouldn't. Not yet anyway. It wouldn't serve any useful purpose to make her more afraid.

He fell silent, enjoying his coffee while his mind turned over the things he should do, and might do, to help protect her. Maybe one of the first things he should do was find a way to speak to the sheriff. But given WITSEC procedures, he doubted Dalton would give him anything useful. No, he guessed he was on his own with this, at least until he had something more than suspicion.

But he was fairly decent on his own. And he was intimately acquainted with his own abilities and weaknesses. After all, he'd spent twenty years honing those abilities and weeding out those weaknesses.

So the question now was how much he should share with Cory. Should he let her know what had coalesced everything for him? Or should he let it ride to avoid making her any more frightened? That was always a difficult question in WITSEC ops. You needed your protectee to be as cooperative as possible, as helpful as possible, but you didn't want to scare him or her needlessly because that could result in actions born of fear that could endanger the entire operation.

Cory still had her head down, her face concealed. He studied her, trying to see her as a mission, not as a woman who had stirred some long-buried feelings in him.

He needed to gain her confidence, sufficiently that she would trust him if he told her to do something. That was primary. But how? This was no ordinary operation where being bulked-up in body armor and armed to the teeth would do the job.

Well, he couldn't let her know how much she had betrayed by her silences. That would scare her into wondering if she'd left a crumb trail for someone to follow.

Yet, he feared someone had found her. That phone call, he was now certain, had been no innocent prank. Someone was sounding out women who fit a certain profile. Waiting to see if something changed after the call. He could explain it no other way. Certainly you wouldn't warn your intended target if you were certain you had the right one. Instead, and he had done this on an operation or two, you would try to precipitate revealing action.

The person or persons who hunted Cory might still be wondering. That would depend on how many changes the other women who got those calls made. Marsha had adopted a dog, making no secret of the fact that she wanted it for protection.

But what had Cory done?

The rest of the picture slammed into place. She'd taken in a boarder. One who could easily look like a bodyguard.

Cripes. Was he himself the link that had led the hunter to her? That would depend on whether the hunter learned of him before or *after* the phone call, and for security purposes, he had to assume the worst.

The thought sickened him.

But still, sitting right before him was the woman whose trust he needed, a woman who knew nothing about him, and was likely to know nothing about him unless he started opening up the coffins of his past enough that she felt she knew him.

He swore silently, and poured more coffee into his mug. He needed to go totally against his own nature here. Needed to expose himself in ways he never did.

In that regard, this was a very different type of operation. But where to begin?

He cleared his throat, trying to find words. She looked at him immediately, which didn't really help at all. But he had to take the plunge, sort of like jumping out of a helicopter into a stormy sea and falling sixty or more feet into water that had turned into bricks.

Her eyes looked more alert now, pretty brown eyes, naturally soft and warm, especially right now when fear hadn't tightened them.

"I, um, told you I'm not good at making connections."

She nodded, but didn't try to say anything.

"Truth is, I feel like an alien."

Her eyebrows lifted, but her eyes remained warm, and even gentled a bit. "How so?"

Well now, that was hard to explain. But he'd been the one who brought it up. "Because I've been places ordinary people don't go."

She gave another nod, a slow one. "I take it you don't mean geographically."

"No." And leaving it there wasn't going to get this part of his mission done. He could almost hear the vault doors creak as he opened the crypt of feelings he didn't care to share. "I've done things, seen things, survived things most people can't even imagine. I know what I'm capable of in ways most people never will, thank God. And I can't talk about it. Partly because most of it is classified, but partly because no one will understand anyway."

"I can see that."

"The only people who truly understand are the people I served with. And we all have that sense of alienation. Some are proud of it. Maybe even most. But there's a cost."

"I would imagine so."

"So we can't make connections. We try. Then we watch it all go up in smoke. Our wives leave us because we can't talk, our kids feel like we're strangers who just show up from time to time, even parents look at us like they don't know who we are. And they don't. We pretend, try to appear ordinary, but nothing inside us is ever ordinary again. And finally we realize the only people we can truly connect with anymore are our fellow team members."

He watched her eyes glaze with thought as she absorbed what he was saying. "I guess," she said slowly, "I can identify with that just a little bit."

He waited to see if she would volunteer anything more,

but she didn't. So he decided to forge ahead. "I'm not saying this out of self-pity."

"I didn't think you were."

"I'm just trying to explain why I'm so difficult to talk with. Over the years, between secrets I couldn't discuss, and realities I shouldn't discuss, I got so I didn't talk much at all."

She nodded once more. "Did you have a wife? Kids?"

"I was lucky. I watched too many marriages fall apart before I ever felt the urge. That's one closet without skeletons."

"And now your only support group, the rest of your team, has been taken away from you."

He hadn't thought of it that way before, but he realized she was right. "I guess so."

"So what do you do now?"

"I'm trying to work my way into a life without all that, but I'll be honest, I'm having trouble envisioning it."

"I'm..." She hesitated. "I guess I'm having the same kind of problem, generally speaking. I can't seem to figure out where I want to go, either."

He waited, hoping she'd offer more, but she said nothing else, merely sipped her coffee. So he tried a little indirect prompting. "Big changes can do that. You'd think, though, that since I knew I was going to retire I could have planned better."

A perfect opportunity to say her changes had come without time to plan, or even any choices, but she didn't say anything. Which left him to try to find another way in.

For the first time, it occurred to him that talking to him must be as frustrating for others as talking to Cory was for him. Okay, regardless of his reasons for preferring silence, that wasn't going to work this time. If he was right, and he was rarely wrong about things like this, she had to learn to trust him.

But he'd never had to win anyone's trust in this way before. Oh, he'd gained the trust of his team members in training, during operations and eventually even some of it by reputation. But none of those tools were available to him here. A whole new method was needed and he didn't have the foggiest idea how to go about finding it.

Nor, if he was right, did they have months to get to that point.

Maybe he had to keep talking. He sure as hell couldn't think of any other way. The problem was that most of the past twenty years of his life contained so much classified information, and so much that he couldn't share with the uninitiated, that his own memory might as well have been stamped *Top Secret*. And what did you talk about besides the weather if you couldn't refer to your memories?

But then Cory herself opened the door to a place that wasn't classified but that he wished could be. She asked, "Do you have any family?"

His usual answer to that was a flat no. But given his task here, he bit the bullet. "None that I speak to."

"Oh. Why?"

"It was a long time ago." Which meant he ought to be able to elaborate. It had nothing to do any longer with who he was. In fact, he'd removed them almost as cleanly as an amputation.

Then she totally floored him. Before he could decide what to tell her, and what to omit, she said gently, "You were abused, weren't you?"

Little had the power to stun him any longer, but that simple statement did. "What, am I wearing a mark on my forehead?"

She shook her head. "I don't mean to pry. But just a

couple of things you've said… Well, they reminded me of some…people I worked with."

Still hedging her way around her past, while asking about his. The tables had turned, and he'd helped her do it. Didn't mean he had to like it.

"Well, yes," he finally said. "What things did I say?"

"It doesn't matter, really. You're not that child any longer, but there were just some echoes of things I've heard before. Most people wouldn't even notice."

The way most people wouldn't notice her omissions. His estimate of her kicked up quite a few notches. In her own way, she was as observant as he.

She reached for the carafe between them, and poured a little more coffee into her mug. Then she added just a tiny bit of milk. "Sometimes," she said, "I guess things stay with us, even when they've been left far in the past."

"I guess." How could he deny it when she had picked up on something he'd buried a long, long time ago? "Yeah, they were abusive."

"Physically as well as emotionally?"

"Yeah."

"I'm sorry." Her brown eyes practically turned liquid with warmth and concern. "Did that play a part in you becoming a SEAL?"

He was about to deny it, because he had, after all, been out of the house for nearly a year before he joined the navy. But then he realized something, and saw how it dovetailed into what was going on here, and he made a conscious decision to breach a barrier so old and so strong that he was hardly aware of it any longer.

"Yes," he said finally. "In a way I suppose it did."

"How so?"

Well, *he'd* opened the vault. "After I got out of high

school, I couldn't shake them off fast enough. I worked my way through a few jobs, feeling at loose ends. Confused."

"Confused?" She repeated the word, and he could tell she felt the connection to her own situation. He could have waited for her to add something, but he suspected she wouldn't.

"Confused," he said again flatly. "I'd lived most of my life with one goal, to survive and to get away from them. And once I was away, I didn't have a goal anymore. I felt like a stranger to myself. I finally realized that the way I was drifting I wasn't going to get anywhere, so one morning I walked into a recruiter's office. Then I had a goal again, something more than merely surviving. They gave me one."

She nodded. "I can understand that. I really can. I'd like to have a goal again."

He took a gamble, sharing a little more of himself. "When you've lived for so long thinking of yourself in one way, looking at life in one way, and then something dramatic changes, it's like the earth vanishes from beneath your mental feet. Your whole identity can vanish."

"That's exactly how it feels." Her face reflected pain.

"Especially when everything you thought you were was a reflection of the life you were living."

He heard her draw a small, sharp breath. So he plunged on, laying himself out there. "For so long I'd identified myself in opposition to my parents, partly by denying all they told me I was, and partly in reaction against them and everything they did and believed. And all of a sudden I didn't have anything to push against anymore. Any goal to fight for. Well, I'm kind of there again."

Her head jerked up and she looked straight at him. "Because you retired?"

He nodded. "For twenty years, the navy gave me an identity and a goal. Now it's all gone again."

"Oh, Wade," she said quietly. "I know how hard that is."

"Somehow," he said pointedly, "I think you do."

Her eyes widened a shade. Then she confided something for the very first time. "I was...my husband died a little over a year ago. Before I came here. Everything went up in smoke."

Still evasive, but at last a nugget of the truth. He waited, hoping she would say more, but she didn't. And he'd said about all he could stand about himself. Admitted more to her than he had really wanted to about himself. Voiced out loud the struggle he'd been facing for six months now without any success.

God, he felt exposed. And life had taught him that when you exposed yourself this way, all you did was give someone ammunition to use against you.

He could have used a ten-mile run right then, but he fought down the urge to get up and walk away. Only two things stopped him: this woman might be at risk, and he realized he couldn't keep running from himself any longer.

He'd been running an awful long time. All the way back to the age of four. Running inside his head, running with his career, always running.

One of these days he needed to stop, and apparently today was going to be the day.

# Chapter 6

Wade excused himself to go shower. Cory placed the coffee carafe back on the warmer, put the milk away and washed their mugs. She smothered another yawn, considered getting dressed, then discarded the idea. It was just too early to bother, especially when she didn't have anywhere to go.

But she did have a lot to think about. Wandering into her living room, she curled up on one end of the couch, tucking her robe around her legs, and put her chin in her hand thinking over all Wade had shared with her that morning.

She wished she knew what had unlocked his silence but she had to admit it was good to know something about him even if it wasn't a whole lot.

But she wasn't at all surprised to find out he'd been an abused child. Nor did it surprise her to learn that the navy had given him what he needed. Often abused children needed order in their lives, clear-cut rules to follow, after being subjected to the unpredictable whims of mean adults. The regimented lifestyle took away the fear of never knowing what would bring retribution down on their heads.

And apparently he'd needed to take charge at the same time, or he never would have gone into the SEALs. Maybe there'd even been an element of *nobody's ever going to get away with treating me that way again.*

She didn't consider herself an expert, but in eight years of teaching she'd certainly seen enough kids fighting these same battles, and few enough who were willing to talk about it. It was sad how they became coconspirators with their abusers, protecting their tormentors with silence and even outright lies.

And often, even when she thought she had enough to report it to the authorities, nothing came from it. Without physical evidence, as long as the child denied it, there was little enough anyone could do.

The thing that had always struck her, though, was the incalculable emotional damage that must come from being so mistreated by the very people a child by rights ought to be able to trust.

Well, she'd always wondered about that, and now she was looking at it. He seemed to blame his job for his inability to make connections, and perhaps it was responsible in large measure, but she suspected the seeds of the problem lay in his childhood. If you couldn't trust your own parents, who could you trust?

She closed her eyes, chin still in her hand. As always, when confronted with something like this, she wanted to help, but in this case she didn't see how she possibly could. This was a man who must be what? Thirty-eight? Thirty-nine? She couldn't just step in like some delivering angel.

He wouldn't want it, and honestly, she didn't know enough to be much help. The best she could do was listen when he was willing to talk.

He had turned out to be a good case for not judging a book by its cover, though. If her ears hadn't become properly tuned through teaching, she probably would have thought all along that he was a hard, harsh man, sufficient unto himself, needing no one and nothing. That's certainly what he had tried to become, and the image he tried to perpetuate.

And she had to admit she felt a lot more comfortable now knowing that he wasn't the stone monolith he had first seemed.

Listening to him had also made her think about her own situation, and doing so made her squirm a bit. Yes, terrible things had happened to her, and her entire life had changed as a result, but how could she truly excuse her waste of the past year? Terror and trauma could explain only so much. The woman she had once believed herself to be had turned out to be a weakling and a coward.

She gave herself no quarter on that one. Some of it could be excused, but not all of it. After all, look what Wade had managed to achieve out of his own trauma as a child. He may have drifted for nearly a year, but then he'd taken a stand to make something of himself.

She hadn't even tried.

But even as she sat there trying to beat herself up in the hopes that she might regain some sense of purpose or direction, she found herself remembering that episode in the kitchen yesterday, when he had lifted her onto the counter and kissed her.

Oh, man, that had started some kind of internal snowball rolling. Just the memory of those all-too-brief moments was enough to make her clamp her thighs together as the throbbing ache reawakened. She had thought that part of her dead and buried for good, only to discover it could come back to life at the merest touch.

Like a daffodil determined to bloom even though snow still lay on the ground in an icy blanket, her body responded to the memory as surely as the touch. She could only imagine what it might feel like to be claimed by such a man, one so powerful and strong, one so confident in his own desire. Sex with Jim had been good: loving and tender. She couldn't help but feel that the entire experience would be different with Wade: hot and hard.

And maybe that's what she needed now, someone to push her past all the invisible lines she had drawn around herself, someone to knock her off center enough to emerge from her cocoon.

Because she sure as hell needed some kind of kick.

Wade returned downstairs eventually, waking her from a half doze where dreams of hot kisses had collided with inchoate fears, the kind of feeling that something was chasing her, but she couldn't escape it, and the kisses felt like both protection and trap.

Freshly shaven, smelling of soap even from several feet away, he sat facing her. "Sorry, woke you again."

"I didn't want to doze off. If you want some, the coffee should still be hot." The memory of her odd half dream made her cheeks equally hot. She hoped he couldn't see and thought he probably couldn't since she kept the curtains closed, and the early daylight out.

It was time to start opening those curtains. Time to allow the sunlight into her house, something she hadn't yet done in all this time.

She rose at once and went to the pull cord. The instant her hand touched it, Wade barked, "Don't."

With that single command, he drove all her resolutions

out of her head and brought the crippling fear back in a rush.

She froze, feeling her knees soften beneath her. She wanted some anger, even just one little flare of it, but it failed to come. Instead she reached for the wall beside the curtain, propping herself against it and closing her eyes.

When her voice emerged, it was weak. "Why?"

"I'm sorry." As if he sensed the storm that had just torn through her, leaving her once again gutted by fear, he came to her, slipping his arm around her waist, and guiding her back to the couch. "I'm sorry," he said again as he helped her sit, and sat beside her. He kept her hand, holding it between both of his, rubbing it with surprising gentleness.

This had to stop, Cory thought. This had to stop. One way or another, she had to find a way to get rid of this fear. Else how was she ever going to do anything again? "I can't keep doing this," she said to Wade, her voice thin. "I can't."

"Keep doing what?"

"Being afraid all the time. And I was just starting to do things to fight it back. Like letting you move in here. Like helping Marsha yesterday. Like opening the damn curtains for the first time in a year! And you told me to stop. Why? *Why?*"

At least she didn't dissolve into tears, but she felt on the brink of it. Ever since that phone call, she'd been teetering as she hadn't teetered in a long time. Before that she'd lived in a steady state at least, even if it was one of grief and fear.

Wade surprised her by drawing her into his arms and holding her. "I'm sorry," he murmured, and stroked her hair gently. "I'm sorry."

"After…after…" The thought fled before a renewed

rush of terror as something struck her. "What do you know?" she asked on a whisper. "What do you know that I don't?"

His hand hesitated, then resumed stroking her hair. "I'm not sure I know anything."

"Tell me!" Her hands balled into fists, and she pounded one of them against his chest, not hard, but enough to make a point. That chest yielded to her fist about as much as cement.

He sighed, tightening his arms around her.

"Wade, don't do this to me. You either know something or you don't."

When his answer seemed slow in coming, she stiffened, ready to pull away. "You can't do this," she said, anger beginning to replace fear, and weakness with strength. "You can't! You can't just waltz into my life and then do things to make me afraid all over again. Not without a reason. I won't stand for it."

"All right. Just keep in mind this may be meaningless."

"Just tell me."

"That man we met at the store yesterday morning? The one we ran into later in the aisle?"

"Yes? What about him?"

"Early this morning I realized he was driving the car behind the woman who waved to us as we were walking back to the house."

She hardly remembered the incident and had to make herself think back. Yes, a man had driven past them, right after that woman. She tipped her head back, trying to look at him. "But it was a different car."

"Yes, it was. But it was the same man. Maybe he just owns two cars."

No matter how hard she tried, she couldn't remember

the face of the man in the car during their walk. "How can you be sure? I can't even remember what he looked like."

"Training. If I hadn't gotten so lazy over the last six months, I'd have picked up on it right away. And he might just have two cars. A lot of folks do."

He looked down at her at last, his obsidian eyes like chips of stone. "I can't ignore it. Coincidence or not, I *cannot* ignore it."

She bit her lip, then said, "That's what made you come down so early this morning. Why you went out to jog. You were looking for him."

He nodded. "I didn't find him."

"So it could be coincidence."

"Maybe."

She shook her head a little, trying to sort through a bunch of conflicting thoughts. Finally she came up with one question. "That phone call couldn't be part of it, could it? I mean…" She wanted to believe it was all random chance, but the phone call kept rearing up in her mind, some part of her insisting it was no prank. "It doesn't make sense. Why call me if you know where I am?"

"Because maybe you don't know exactly which of a handful of women is your target."

"And how would that prove a damn thing?"

He loosened his hold on her, giving her space, but she didn't move away. She didn't want to. Odd considering that he was busy ripping her newfound courage to shreds. Not that it had been much to begin with.

He spoke finally. "Sometimes the only way to identify a target is to do something that makes them take a revealing action."

She searched his face, but it remained unreadable. "You've done that?"

"A couple of times."

"It works?"

"It did for me."

"But I haven't done anything since the call! So that can't be what's going on."

"Maybe. Maybe not."

"Stop being so elliptical. Just tell me what you're thinking. Please!"

"I moved in here right before you got the call. What if the person trying to locate you saw me only after the call?"

Her stomach sank, and right along with it her heart. "Bodyguard," she whispered. Then she had another horrifying thought. "Marsha got a dog."

"If I were them, I doubt I'd pay much attention to a dog."

She was feeling sicker by the second. "No. Especially not when they could trace her back if they want to. If they can."

"Can they?"

In that question she heard the million unanswered questions her own life had become. She had as good as admitted what was going on here. And he had apparently figured out plenty on his own. Now what? Tell the truth, or leave the lies hanging out there. The omissions. The secrets.

Then she had another thought. "What if..." This one really sickened her. So much so she wrenched away from him and jumped up from the couch. She backed away, wrapping her arms around herself, staring at him, feeling horror start to grow.

"What if I'm the one hunting you?" he asked. "Good question. Call the sheriff right now. Tell him to come get me. Tell him whatever you want."

"And then what?"

"And then I'll leave. I'll be gone from this county as fast as I can pack my duffel."

Did she want that? No...no... Not if he was who he was really supposed to be. "You know too much about me."

"Lady, I know nothing about you. I've guessed some things, but you sure as hell haven't told me anything."

"What did you guess?"

He passed a hand over his face. "Will it scare you if I get up and pace? I'm not really good at holding still unless I have to."

She waved a hand, indicating permission. God, when he stood he seemed to fill the entire room.

He started pacing, but slowly, taking care not to come too close to her. "You know I noticed how afraid you are."

"Yes."

"Well, I noticed some other things, too, and last night it just all kind of came together for me. The way when you talk about things from your past you hesitate and then skip anything that might actually give away where you lived before. I also noticed that when you got scared by the phone call you turned to the sheriff."

"What does that tell you?"

He looked at her. "That you're scared and on the run from some threat that still haunts you. But you're not running from the law, or your first response wouldn't have been to call Gage Dalton."

She nodded stiffly. "Okay."

"I noticed the security system. You can't afford it."

"No," she admitted.

"I've been involved in WITSEC ops overseas."

"WITSEC?"

"Witness security. Witness protection."

"Oh…my…God…" She sank onto the rocking chair, arms still tightly wrapped around her.

"All the signs are there for someone who can read them. Which most people can't. It took me more than a day to figure it out, so don't worry that you've tipped off everyone in the county. I'm sure you haven't. But it's the only picture that fits. Am I wrong?"

She shook her head stiffly. "It was that easy?"

"Actually, you made it very hard. Like I said, I didn't glom on to it immediately. But when I put a few things together, it was the only explanation I could think of. The alternative was to think you're just crazy, and you're not crazy, Cory."

She felt numb, almost out of her own body, with shock. This man had figured her out so fast, and yet he said it had taken him too long. How did that add up?

But if he'd figured it out, how many others had? No one, he said. But could she safely believe it?

"Trust me," he said, "it wouldn't occur to anyone not familiar with the protocols. You don't give anything away."

"I…find that hard to believe, now."

"Well, believe it. WITSEC is not the first thing that would occur to anyone about you. It would probably be the last."

"Why?"

"Because no one would suspect you of being a criminal, even if they suspect you have some secrets."

"I'm not a criminal!"

"I know that. It's obvious. And since everyone thinks that only criminals get witness protection, you're even more covered. Very well covered."

Her eyes burned and she felt hollow as she looked at him. "What now?" she asked, a bare whisper.

"Well, all I have is a suspicion. But you can choose how to act on it. Call the sheriff, I'll tell him everything I noticed about the guy. Call the Marshals and they'll move you again. Or...I can try to protect you until we get something solid."

She'd already made up her mind she didn't want to move again. Once was enough. What few tenuous connections she had managed to make here were more than she wanted to sacrifice. She couldn't face another blank slate in a blank town, couldn't face having to start all over again, small though her start here had really been. After all, there was Emma, Marsha, Gage, Nate and Marge Tate. While she hadn't exactly gotten close, she had come to know them a bit. And she discovered she wanted to know them even better.

She raised her eyes to his, resolve steadying her. "I'm not running again."

He nodded. "I kind of decided the same thing this morning."

She nodded slowly. "I guess you did." Her decision made, her muscles began to uncoil slowly, one by one. "I guess I need to tell you the story."

"Cory, you don't have to tell me a damned thing. I can work this without knowing. Your secrets can remain your secrets. But I gather, since you didn't recognize the guy at the store, that he's not someone you're afraid of."

"No. Actually...I saw only one man. The man who killed my husband and shot me."

"Shot you?" He stopped short.

She nodded, and for some reason she didn't understand, she opened her robe and tugged her pajama top up enough to reveal the scar across her midriff. "He killed my baby, too."

He swore, a word she wasn't used to hearing, and the

next thing she knew he'd gathered her up off the chair and was carrying her through the house toward her bedroom. There he laid her down on the queen-size bed, and stretched out beside her. Without another word, he drew her into a close embrace, as if he wanted to surround her with the shield of his body. As if he wanted to shelter her from it all.

But nothing could. She stared blindly at his chin as her head rested on his upper arm, feeling as if a wind had blown through her and left her empty in every way, empty of her past, empty of her hopes and dreams, empty of feeling.

Something in her had died all over again.

In the hollowness that seemed to engulf her, she heard her own voice. It sounded dreamy, disconnected, as if it belonged to someone else and she wasn't in control. And maybe she wasn't.

"I didn't really grieve about the baby," she heard herself say. "I'd just found out that morning. Not enough time for it to become real."

"Mmm." A sound to let her know he was listening, indicating no reaction whatever. She didn't want a reaction. She couldn't have handled one just then.

"What *was* real was that when I woke up from surgery they told me that the only part of Jim I had left was gone, too. I miscarried because of the trauma."

"I'm sorry."

"I was…I was at the best and brightest point of my life that night. The happiest. I had Jim, we were going to have a baby. Maybe no one is entitled to that much happiness."

"Everyone is entitled to that kind of happiness."

"Really? Even you?"

He didn't answer, his silence speaking volumes.

"We went out for dinner to celebrate the news, came

home and…made love. I was so happy I couldn't even sleep. And then some son of a bitch came through our door and took it all away with a gun."

He murmured something, but she didn't try to make it out. She didn't care. Numbness still wrapped her like cotton wool.

"I saw the man. They couldn't find him, though, couldn't identify him. We think…they think…he was working for a drug gang that Jim was about to bring in indictments against. A hired gun, probably. They put me in protection from the instant I got to the hospital. They wouldn't even let me go to Jim's funeral."

His arms tightened a bit, but he said nothing.

"Then, after three months in a safe house, they told me I had to relocate because the word on the street was there was a contract on me because I could identify Jim's murderer."

"Not penny-ante criminals then."

"No. Sometimes I think they were bigger fish than even Jim realized."

"Maybe so."

"There wasn't even a threat beforehand. No warning of any kind. The grand-jury testimony was sealed, the indictments were going to be sealed until they'd rounded everyone up. Maybe there was a leak from somewhere. No one seemed to know. I'll probably never know."

"So three months in a safe house, and then the beginning of the journey to nowhere."

"First, first they did a little plastic surgery. I had a nose job. Just enough to make me look different if anyone had a photo of me. My hair…I have to color it. I wear it differently now. Not big changes."

"Big enough changes. The nose especially. Minimal change, maximum impact."

"That's what they said. Change a nose and you change the whole face."

"That must have been hard for you."

"Even now I sometimes jump when I look in a mirror. Anyway, they moved me through three towns before the nose job. After that, it was another six towns. We'd stay for a while, then they'd pack me up and move me again. They said they were making sure nobody could follow me."

"That's right."

"So you've done that part, too?"

"I've done it all, from the moving to the safe-house protection. Of course, I had the disadvantage of having to protect a couple of really bad guys. Sometimes it seems hardly worth the trouble."

"But it is, right?"

"If they have enough information, yes. In your case, it would have been an honor."

She reached up with one hand and touched his chin. At once he tipped his head to look at her. "I hated it."

"I imagine so."

"But they were really doing everything they possibly could for me. Even while I hated it, I understood it. They went out of their way for me."

"Because you were innocent."

"Because my husband was an assistant U.S. attorney. Because he was one of theirs. I don't kid myself that I would have gotten the same kind of care except for Jim. The only man I could put behind bars is the man who killed a federal prosecutor."

Something in his dark eyes seemed to soften just a hair, but he didn't argue with her, probably because he knew she was right.

"Those kinds of resources," she said, "don't get spent on just anybody. I could have witnessed almost any other murder, been the only one able to identify the killer, and I'd have been on my own before long."

"Seems like you're kind of on your own now."

"That's the way it works."

He nodded. "Most of the time. Are you angry about that?"

"That I got first class instead of coach? How could I be angry about that? What I'm angry about is that every single thing I cared about was stripped away from me. My family, my friends, my career. Sometimes I get angry at myself for letting them take me away."

"Be sensible. What good would it possibly have done to get yourself killed?"

"It might have spared me the limbo I've been living in."

He sighed and cupped her cheek with his warm hand. "Now that's crazy talk. Somehow we'll get this guy and then you can get on with your life."

"Can I? I'm not so sure of that. I was supposed to be safe ever since I got here, but I haven't spent one hour of one day without looking over my shoulder."

"All I can tell you is that things may be coming to a head finally. And that I'm trained for this kind of stuff. And that the last year…Cory, think about all you went through. Of course you couldn't get your bearings, especially when you had good reason to be terrified."

"Apparently so, since I seem to have been found."

He fell silent for a half minute, then said, "You're going to hate me for this."

"For what?"

"Maybe it's a good thing you've been found. Maybe we can deal with this mess for once and for all. Maybe we can get your life back."

"I don't exactly have a life to get back anymore."

"Maybe you could even go home and resume your career."

"I don't know about that. I'm not sure I want to." She was sorry then, sorry because the numbness wore off suddenly and she started feeling again.

And what she felt was a pain deeper and wider than the Grand Canyon. When she started to cry, he just gathered her closer.

As if that would help. As if anything could help.

# Chapter 7

He wiped her tears gently away when she finally quieted. For a long time he just held her, but finally he spoke. "We have to talk about how to deal with this."

"What can we possibly do?

"Well, I'll have to think about that some, but we've still got to talk. We have to sort through your options and my options, and see what we can come up with. There's a lot I can do, but I don't usually plan entire operations by myself."

"Teamwork?"

"Yes. And you're my team. And the sheriff, too. We've got to talk this all over with him."

"I don't want to! What if he calls the Marshals? I don't want to do that again."

"Easy now. I'm sure we can convince Gage not to do that. But as good as I may be, I'm still just one man, Cory. We're going to need some help."

She pressed her face into his shoulder, hating all of this, from the fear that tingled along her spine to the sense of being trapped in a nightmare. Why couldn't she have even an hour of forgetfulness? Was that so much to ask?

Then he shifted her, so that she lay even closer to him. His hand began to run over her back, in steady, soothing circles. At least she thought he meant them to be soothing, but after a few minutes they had a totally different effect. Their passionate kiss yesterday had made her aware of her own needs again, and it didn't take long for her body to remind her that there was still something good in life, something that could be hers for the asking. Something that would make her forget.

But forgetfulness quickly took a backseat to a slowly building heat. Even if her mind and heart quailed, her body wanted to spring back to life, to grasp it with both hands and revel in it.

The softest of sighs escaped her, and she tried to wiggle closer, to say with her body what she could not with words.

His hand paused. As soon as she realized he must have received her silent message, she caught and held her breath, torn between an impulse to pull away and hide, and an almost excruciating hope that he wouldn't turn her away.

She should run. Now. Because she couldn't handle the rejection. Not now. Not after all she had exposed about herself.

*Turn away* now, *don't give him the chance to say no.*

But her body refused to obey her brain. It wanted something primal, something more elemental, an affirmation of life that bypassed all those messed-up circuits in her brain.

His hand left her back. She tensed in expectation of the rejection. But instead he caught her chin and turned her face up so they were looking at one another, only inches apart. His dark eyes searched hers, then moved over her face, as if seeking an answer to some question.

Then he swooped in like a bird of prey and took her mouth in a kiss that stunned her with its intensity, as if he wanted to draw her very soul out of her.

Oh, he knew how to kiss. His tongue mated with hers in a rhythm that exactly matched the pulsing it set off in her body. Fireworks sparkled along her nerve endings, making every inch of her so sensitive that the merest brush of clothing against her skin seemed overwhelmingly sensual and sexual.

He shifted, tugging both her legs between his, so they were locked together and her throbbing center was out of reach even as it grew heavy and aching with need.

All from a kiss.

Her body wanted to fight the imprisonment until she felt his hardness against her belly. She understood then. He wanted her every bit as much as she wanted him, but he would make her wait, slow her down, force patience where she felt none.

And that understanding made her relax into his arms, and let him have his way. *No need to rush.* No need at all. Somehow that freed her in a way desire alone couldn't have.

He continued to hold her close with one arm as he kissed her, but his other hand began to wander. He slipped it under her robe, leaving only her pajamas in the way, and stroked her side from breast to thigh, to the point where his leg trapped hers, then swept it up again, slowly…oh, so slowly.

And as it returned upward, it slid beneath her pajama top, and she gasped. She arched a little, breaking the kiss as she felt his callused palm touch her bare skin. He stayed there for a while, drawing slow, lazy circles on her middle while his mouth claimed hers again, this time more gently, echoing the touch of his fingers.

Impatience started to build in her again, causing her to squirm a bit against his bondage, but he didn't release her. Her breasts ached for a touch, a kiss, until she thought she would go out of her mind from the longing.

Yet still he withheld it.

Tearing her mouth from his, she gasped for air, then reached with one hand to undo the buttons of his shirt. If he wasn't going to give her more, she would take more.

He didn't stop her when she pulled open his shirt and pressed her palm at last to his chest. She thought she even heard a deep sound of pleasure escape him as she began to trace the contours of those hard muscles, glorying in the smoothness of his skin, in the ripples across his belly, in the small points of his nipples. Exquisite. Perfect. As much a feast for her hands as he had been for her eyes.

Then without warning, his hands gripped her around her waist, he freed her from the prison of his legs and leaving her almost dizzy, he lifted her over him, so that she straddled his hips.

A groan escaped her as he tugged her down until her moist yearning depths met his hardness through layers of denim and cotton. What was he doing? She needed to get rid of the clothing that interfered.

But when she reached for the snap of his jeans, he stopped her and murmured roughly, "Just ride me, Cory."

She didn't know what he meant until his hands gripped her hips again and he moved her against him. All of a sudden those layers of fabric didn't seem to matter. Her hips helplessly rocked against him, demanding a solution to the problem of need.

And as she rocked, he slipped his hands up under her nightshirt and cupped her breasts, rubbing his thumbs over her nipples.

He might as well have plugged her into an electric socket. Shocks zinged through her, setting her alight, then zipped to her center, creating an ache that made her forget everything, everything except her need.

"That's the way…" He groaned the words, urging her on, tormenting her even as he encouraged her to ride the cresting wave. And somehow, by keeping them both clothed, he had set her free in an unexpected way.

Set her free to take what she wanted as she rubbed herself against him over and over. Set her free to give in to her need without thought of anything or anyone other than herself.

Free to be.

Free to ride the crest of the wave all the way until she tumbled wildly into the warm waters below.

And knew peace.

She lay on Wade's chest, his arms around her as aftershocks made her tremble. Her legs sprawled on either side of him, leaving her open, and each aftershock caused her to tighten them just a bit against his hips.

She felt more safe, more secure and more relaxed than she had since…the shooting. And she couldn't even rustle up a smidgen of guilt about it.

Well, except that she didn't know if Wade had enjoyed it quite as much as she had, didn't know if he'd found completion himself. And had no way to ask.

Silly, after what they had just shared, an experience all the more exhilarating because of the way he had brought it about, that she should feel a bit shy. But there it was.

But oh, she never would have believed that having sex

while fully clothed could actually enhance the experience, could arouse her so much, could give her such a sense of primitive freedom. In a way, she supposed, it had been an updated version of dragging her away to a cave by her hair. Little finesse, a lot of hunger, and *bam!*

He'd lingered just long enough for her inhibitions to weaken, and then he'd forced her to shed them all. Quick, hot and ready.

And damn, it felt good.

He moved at last, just a bit, lifting a hand to stroke the back of her head, then wind a strand of her hair around his finger.

"You okay?" he asked gruffly.

"I'm fine," she murmured. "You?"

"Pretty amazed, actually."

At that she lifted her head and looked at him. His hard face looked softer now, and even his obsidian eyes seemed less like rock and more like deep waters. "How so?"

"I couldn't begin to explain."

She laid her cheek on his chest again. "Some things beggar words, I guess."

"Maybe so." He released the strand of her hair, and ran a fingertip along the curve of her jaw. "Were you a teacher, before?"

This man had a gift for putting a few pieces together into complete a puzzle, so she guessed it shouldn't have surprised her that he had figured that out. "Why do you ask?"

"Something you said. Well, actually, something you started to say and never finished. You caught yourself just as you started to say the word."

"And you finished it."

"I do that sometimes."

"God, you're incredible. It's like you read minds."

"I'm just observant. You don't have to tell me."

"No, it's okay. I was a teacher. Maybe I'll teach again someday."

"Was there a reason they didn't just get you a certificate here?"

"They felt it would leave too much of a trail." And here was reality, intruding again. She almost wanted to beat her fist on something.

"Sorry, guess I'm ruining the moment."

She must have grown tenser, she thought. In some way he'd picked up on her reaction. He was amazing. In so many ways. Jim had been a sensitive guy, but not this sensitive. "No, I can't hide for long from reality. Not now," she admitted finally. "Not when there may be a threat."

"No." A word of agreement.

Her stomach chose that moment to growl loudly. No more breaks for her today, she thought almost ruefully.

"I think," Wade said after a moment, "that you ought to take a shower while I go make us some breakfast."

"You're going to do the cooking?"

"I told you I know some basics. I may not be able to turn out that pasta thing you managed last night, but I can make a mean scrambled egg, and I can cook it with anything from sunlight, to a flameless ration heater, to a candle to a stove."

"I recommend the stove."

"Since it's available."

She lifted her head and looked at him again. "How do you cook with sunlight?"

"We carry mirrors for signaling. All you have to do is set it up right."

She nodded. "Someday you'll have to show me."

He rolled then, dumping her off him onto the bed. He smiled, actually smiled down at her as he raised himself on one elbow. "Shower," he repeated. "I'll go make some edible scrambled eggs."

Then he gave her a quick hard kiss and was gone.

For the first time in forever, Cory thought about what she was putting on. Ordinarily she grabbed a uniform from her closet, or just a shirt and jeans, not caring which. But this morning she dithered over whether she should wear a denim skirt, the brown plaid shirt with the piped yoke, or a plainer polo shirt.

Finally she told herself to stop being ridiculous, pulled on fresh jeans—in Florida jeans were rarely worn except when it was cool, but here everyone wore them even if it was hot—and the gold polo shirt. She even added a bit of lipstick and mascara, from among the few personal possessions she'd been able to bring with her: nothing that wouldn't fit into a suitcase.

Good smells reached her as soon as she opened her bedroom door. Apparently Wade had added some bacon to the menu from the groceries he had bought yesterday, and from the aroma she could tell he'd brewed fresh coffee. Not only a second cup today, but a second pot. Now that was an extravagance she hadn't enjoyed in far too long.

When she entered the kitchen, she found the table already set. The bacon was draining on a paper towel over a plate on the table, and a stack of toast stood on the counter beside the toaster, already buttered.

"You can cook," she said with surprise.

"Told you. What do you think happens when we're at some small firebase on our own? We take turns, and God help the guy who can't even make a decent breakfast."

A little laugh escaped her.

"And here it's easy. You even have a toaster. Take a seat. I'll bring you coffee."

She sat, saying, "I thought you guys had prepackaged meals. What are they called?"

"MREs. Meals, Ready-to-Eat. Three lies in three letters. I won't give you any of the slang names for them."

"But you cooked anyway?"

"When we move, we move fast and travel light. Try to live off the land. Besides, what you eat affects how you smell, so it's best to eat local diet as much as possible."

She noticed his consistent use of the present tense, and wondered if he really found it that hard to put his years as a SEAL in the past, or if the present situation had just put him back in the mental mode as if he'd never left.

"I never would have thought of that," she said as he joined her at the table with the toast and eggs.

The eggs were perfectly cooked, not too dry or moist, though he evidently hadn't whipped them. But why would that occur to him, considering he had done most of his cooking in the field? He'd spiced them with just a hint of cayenne, too, making them more savory.

"Perfect," she said, complimenting him.

One corner of his mouth lifted in a smile. "Thanks. I hate overdone eggs. I'll eat them, but I won't like it."

For a man who said he didn't know how to converse, he was doing a darn good job of it. Maybe something in him had begun to open up, too, as it had inside her.

Almost as soon as she had the thought, he clammed up again. They ate breakfast in silence and hardly said a word as they washed up afterward.

But then, after they moved back into the shadowed living room, he said, "I'm going to call the sheriff."

And ugly reality came crashing back down.

Wade called Gage then excused himself to jog around the block. He didn't say why he was going, but Cory figured it out without having to ask: he was going to make sure the guy he'd noticed yesterday wasn't hovering around. She spent the time pretending to tidy up the house, although all she really needed to do was some dusting. She'd done all her major housework just a few days ago, and while the dust hadn't really built up since then, it gave her an excuse to keep moving, and moving seemed like a good way to hold her fears at bay. Barely.

Wade returned to the house at the same time Gage arrived. They entered together, Gage in civvies, and joined Cory in the living room. Before she could even greet Gage or put down her dustrag, Wade said, "I didn't see him."

Cory wasn't sure that eased her mind at all, given what Wade suspected. She dropped the rag on the table, brushed her hand quickly against her jeans, then shook Gage's hand and invited him to sit. "Coffee?"

He shook his head. "I'm fine. Thanks, Cory. So let's cut to the chase. Wade said next to nothing except you needed to see me."

Cory nodded, then sank slowly onto the Boston rocker. Gage took the easy chair again, and Wade the end of the couch nearest to her. She looked at Wade. "You explain. Please."

"Okay." Wade leaned forward, resting his elbows on his splayed knees, and folded his hands. "I knew from the outset Cory had something to be afraid of. I was here when she got that call, after all, the one she called you about."

Gage nodded. Cory noted he wasn't giving a thing away. He wasn't likely to speak a word until he was certain who knew what, and what they thought was going on. Protecting her secrets.

"Anyway, I won't bore you with all the irrelevant details, unless you think you need them. I've been on WITSEC operations overseas, and by early this morning I realized that Cory must be in Witness Protection."

Gage immediately stiffened. "I don't think…"

"Relax," Wade said. "No one else would guess. I figured it out because I was here, I could see the fear, and some of her omissions were glaring, to say the least."

Gage swore and looked at Cory. "I'm sorry. I never would have brought Wade here if I'd ever thought someone would figure this out."

"It's okay," Cory said. "I'm not upset that he knows. Far from it. And honestly, I think he's right when he says no one else would guess. He figured it out because he had the experience to put the pieces together."

"I hope so," Gage said flatly. Right now he wasn't looking too friendly.

Wade appeared untroubled by the reaction. Or maybe he had just gone back to his inner fortress. Cory surprised herself by hoping like hell that he hadn't. She didn't want him to go back to that. She kind of liked the man he'd revealed himself to be, even though he had as yet revealed little.

"Anyway," Wade continued with little expression, "I also figured out why someone might have made that phone call, and I remembered something I would have caught on to immediately if I hadn't spent the last six months trying to lose most of what I learned as a SEAL."

"And that is?"

"First let me explain a method we used a time or two in operations. You don't always have a clear idea of who your target is. Sometimes you don't have a photo, or even a decent description. So what we would do was try to scare a group of potential targets, then watch who took the most revealing action."

Gage nodded slowly. "So you're saying you don't think that phone call was a prank."

"It might well not be. And the reason I'm suspicious is because we saw the same guy at two different places yesterday. He followed us into the parking lot at the grocery, then we ran into him again in the aisle."

"That doesn't mean anything."

"That alone wouldn't. However, when we were walking home from the park together yesterday afternoon, I saw the guy again. Driving a different car down the street out front."

"Hell." Gage scratched his head almost irritably.

"I realize, of course, that some people have more than one car. I realize that call may indeed have been a prank. But when you put it all together with Cory's being in protection because she's the only person who can identify the man who murdered her husband, it doesn't pay to ignore coincidence."

"No. No, it doesn't. But what would you say is the revealing action Cory took? Because I don't see that she did a thing."

"Except take me in. And the guy who's watching might not have seen me arrive before the call. Actually no reason he should have, because he wouldn't have been looking for telltales until *after* the call…and I arrived basically right before it."

Gage nodded slowly. "It's possible."

"The thing is," Wade continued, "if you assume he's got his eye on, oh, say half a dozen women who've moved here sometime over the last year, and he has to watch all of them, he's going to be looking around at one after another to see who did what after the phone call. And after the call he sees two things: Cory and her friend Marsha go to the pound and pick out a dog for Marsha. That might have been enough to point a finger at Marsha except that then Cory comes home and a very short time later she emerges to go to the grocery store with me."

"And you could easily look like a bodyguard."

Cory spoke. "I think Wade is right, Gage. Especially when you consider that I not only suddenly have Wade living here, but we went shopping together. Ordinarily when people do that, they have a long-term relationship of some kind. But Wade wasn't in my life until the day before yesterday. In fact, when I look back at it, it could easily have appeared that I was doing the shopping and Wade was just *there*."

"Okay," Gage said. "And then you saw him again in the afternoon. In a different car."

"And he didn't even glance at us," Wade remarked, "while the woman in the car ahead of him smiled and waved."

"Most folks in Conard County smile and wave. We're pretty sure someone is an outsider when they don't." He rubbed his chin then looked at Cory.

"But you can't identify him as the man who killed your husband?"

"No, he didn't look anything like that man. I'd have noticed instantly if he had."

Gage cocked one eyebrow and looked at them both. "You know how thin this is?"

"Very," Wade said immediately.

"But it's still not something I can overlook. Give me a minute to think."

For an instant, crazily, Cory heard the *Jeopardy* music in her head. Where had that come from? She looked at Wade and saw a man who was infinitely capable of waiting when necessary, one who might prefer to be moving, but one who could also sit as still as a statue when he chose. He chose to be a statue right now.

Finally Gage spoke. "Okay. The way I see it is that while we can't be sure, Wade is making a good point about revealing actions. The guy who is after Cory may not know her appearance has been changed. They don't often do that in Witness Protection, but given that he can't find anyone who matches her appearance exactly, that kind of provocation would make sense, assuming he somehow found out where she is. And the only way I can think that he would have learned that is if he got the info from someone who works for the Marshals."

Cory's heart skipped a beat then climbed right into her throat. "I didn't even think of that," she whispered hoarsely.

Gage's dark eyes turned her way. "It's been a year, Cory, so it's obvious the Marshals succeeded in making sure no one followed you. So the only way this guy could have any idea you're here is if someone in the program talked. Some kind of leak."

"My God," she whispered. Her skin started to crawl with fear and anxiety again. "What else might he know?"

Gage shook his head. "I don't know, but if Wade is right about that call, then he didn't manage to find out your new name. So whatever someone leaked, it was minimal, or this guy would have your name and address."

"Yes, that's true."

"And it would be my guess that you didn't follow the usual protocol of using the same first name you had before, along with a last name that starts with the same initial, or he'd just as good as have your new name and address."

"No, they told me that's what most people do but one of the Marshals…" Her voice broke, then steadied. "One of the Marshals was a good friend of my husband's. He seemed more worried than the rest, and he was the one who suggested I come up with a totally different name."

"Did you?" Wade asked suddenly. "Totally different? Or could there be a link between your name now and your past?"

Cory bit her lip. "My mother's name was Cory. And her maiden name was McFarland."

Wade looked at Gage. "He could find that out, now that he thinks he might have located her."

Gage nodded. "All too easily. Assuming he bothers to look."

"Why wouldn't he look?" Cory asked, her heart still beating a nervous tattoo.

"Because, assuming this guy does indeed know where you are, he may feel he's already got all the information he needs. I can't read his mind, Cory. I just know we have to take steps."

"What kind of steps? Are you going to call the Marshals?"

Gage shook his head. "Why in the name of all that's holy would I call them? If this isn't just some kind of weird coincidence, then we're dealing with an organization that has already leaked information about you. They're the last ones I'm going to call now. Unless that's what you want me to do."

Cory shook her head quickly. "No. No. I don't want to run again. I can't do that again." Her entire soul seemed to be screaming that another round of running and hiding would break her forever. Clenching her fists, she said again, "No."

Gage's face gentled. "Not even to save your life?"

"What life? If I don't make a stand now, I'll never have one. I'm tired of always being frightened, of always looking over my shoulder. This guy is a killer and I'm the only one who can put him behind bars. If he's found me, then I want to finish it now. I can't...I can't keep living this way. I just can't."

"All right then." Gage stood. "I won't even call the Marshals for a sketch of the murderer. I'm going to send an artist over here to do one just for us. I'd also like a sketch of the guy Wade thinks was following you. Are you up to that, Cory?"

"Definitely." The decision was made. She would stand her ground.

And amazingly, that decision calmed her. The calm probably wouldn't last, but for now it felt wonderful to have finally made the choice. "I'm through letting that guy ruin my life," she said, looking from Gage to Wade. "And frankly, the way I've been living is no life at all. So let's finish it, one way or another."

The police sketch artist turned out to be nothing like Cory had imagined. Esther Nighthawk was a beautiful redhead who wore a long skirt and leaned heavily on a cane. Under one arm, she carried a sketchbook.

"Oh, I just do this to help out," Esther said as Cory invited her into the kitchen so she'd have a table to work on. "I'm a full-time watercolorist, but I enjoy the challenge of doing these sketches for the sheriff."

She settled on the chair facing Cory, and opened her sketchpad to a blank page. Then she pulled a box of drawing pencils from the large woven bag she carried. "I'm sorry we haven't met before. My husband and I live on a ranch—he raises sheep—and I only get to town every couple of weeks for shopping. Or when one of the children needs to come in for something."

"That sounds like a nice life," Cory said almost wistfully.

"It is." Esther's gaze softened a bit. "My life sure changed radically after I met Craig. Before then I spent most of my time hiding."

"From what?"

"Life. I had myself convinced that my art was all that mattered, but basically I was just afraid of a whole bunch of things. *Neurotic* would probably be a good word."

"And now?"

"Now I love every minute of every day." Esther smiled. "So, you're going to help me draw a picture of a man Gage seems to be worried about?"

"Yes. I'll try, anyway."

"You talk, I'll draw."

So Cory closed her eyes for a minute, and tried to summon her memory of the man who killed Jim. "It's hard," she said after a moment. "You know how faces seem to skate away when you concentrate on them?"

"I know. That's why you're not going to concentrate. You're going to give me one detail to start with. I'll draw it, and you watch. As you watch me, tell me what's right and what's not. It'll work. Trust me."

So that's what Cory did. She started with the general shape of the guy's head, and after a few erasures she decided it was correct. Then a nose, and that needed only three iterations. Little by little, the image built, and Esther was right, it was easier to say when something was wrong than to give an exact description of what was right.

A half hour later and she was looking at an eerily familiar face, one she couldn't have pulled out of her memory any other way.

"That's him," she said. "You couldn't possibly get any closer."

Esther nodded, smiling. "It's never as hard as people think it will be."

"Only because you're such a good artist."

Wade joined them, and together he and Cory helped create a sketch of the man they had met at the grocery.

"This is truly amazing," Cory remarked again as she looked at the second sketch. "I thought I'd forgotten him entirely, but this is him."

"You're very gifted," Wade told Esther. "Very gifted."

Esther laughed. "Keep stroking my ego. More is always better." She began to pack up her materials. "Listen, why don't you come out to the ranch for dinner some night? I'd like a chance to get to know you better, and maybe someday you can tell me what this is all about."

"I'd love that," Cory said immediately, realizing she would. The urge to put down roots here had become almost compulsive since just a few days ago. It was as if warning flags had started to pop up in her psyche, telling her that if she continued on her current course she might as well die.

And along with all those warning flags, a desire to start making connections again, a real life again, pushed her.

Possibly into a very dangerous place, the dangerous place she'd spent more than a year hiding from.

Cory said goodbye to Esther at the door, then stepped back away from the opening as Wade ushered the woman to her car.

"Lock up and set the alarm after me," he murmured as he passed. "I'm going to scout a bit before I come back."

She did as told, then went to sit in the living room and wait. How had she survived the past year living this way? Waiting for a doom that never came, too afraid to lead any real kind of life, trying to be invisible even at her job.

With absolute certainty, she knew she couldn't return to that way of life. She'd been dying by inches for too long. She couldn't do it anymore. No way.

And if that meant possibly sticking her head into a noose, then that was what she would do.

Wade returned about twenty minutes later, quieting then resetting the alarm before he joined her.

"You're going to go crazy," she said when he sat beside her.

"I am? Why?"

"Because I just looked in the mirror."

"Meaning?"

She gave a little shake of her head. "Inside this house is limbo. I sit here doing next to nothing, worrying, grieving, afraid. You're going to go nuts locked in here with me."

"I see." He drummed his fingers briefly on the arm of the couch. "I won't go crazy. I've been known to sit in hides for days on end waiting for the right moment, or the target, to appear. I can do it."

"Well, I'm tired of it. I was just sitting here wondering how I'd managed to do nothing for so long."

"Aww, Cory," he said quietly. "Give yourself a break. You went through a terrible trauma, and then you got dumped on a foreign shore where almost nothing was familiar anymore. You needed time. You took it."

"You're very generous."

"Just calling it the way I see it. If you'd lost your husband but been allowed to remain with your friends and family, to keep your job, you could have coped with your grief better. If you hadn't lost your husband but had simply been obliged to move, you would have coped with that, too."

"So sure?"

"I've watched your transformation over the last two days. I'm sure. What's more, I think you need to cut yourself some slack because you experienced two major traumas, both of them stressful to the extreme. And then you had a killer to fear. Most people would have dug a hole and pulled it in after themselves."

"That's basically what I did."

"But look at you now. For whatever reason, you've reached the point where you're ready to take action. But that doesn't mean the time you took to hide and lick your wounds was wrong."

She would never have imagined this man could be so kind. Or that he would be willing to put himself out there the way he had today. He'd seemed so self-contained, so impervious, so…rocklike. Yet while she still felt the almost insurmountable strength in him, she had found a kindness and understanding that seemed like a gift.

It was likely that if she'd ever put herself out there over the past year, she might have found that kind of kindness and understanding from other sources, but she'd been terrified into silence not only by the fact that a killer might be hunting her, but also by all the strictures the Marshals had placed on her. All the warnings. They had meant well, she was sure, but how do you pick up a life that had been so completely and totally interrupted?

"It was like they wanted me to erase myself and start out like a baby all over again."

He nodded. "From their point of view, that seems like the best way to handle it. But it also leaves you without much of a starting point for anything."

"Others are probably more resilient."

"Most of those others didn't see their husbands murdered and lose their baby at the same time."

The stark truth of that bowed her head. She drew a shaky breath, hoping she wouldn't dissolve into tears again.

He slipped his arm around her shoulders and squeezed gently. "Just grant that you've been doing the best you can."

"I want to do better."

"You've made that clear." He paused for a moment, then said, "The way you need to think about the last year or so is that you were wounded. And it takes time to heal. So while you're recovering, there are lots of things your body won't let you do. Or in your case, your mind and emotions. Things that need to rest will rest."

"I hardly think being totally terrified was much of a rest."

"How can you know?"

"What do you mean?" She turned her head to look at him.

"Maybe the fear was a rest from things that were even harder for you to bear."

That drew her up short. She hadn't thought of it that way before, not at all. "Maybe," she said finally. "I know how it's been feeling, though."

"How's that?"

"Like I've been stuck in a quagmire of awful feelings with no way out."

"And now?"

"I see a door. I don't like what might be on the other side. It scares me. But, like I said, I've got to crawl out of this swamp or I'm going to die anyway."

"We'll get you out."

He sounded so confident. She wished she could be as sure. But life offered absolutely no guarantees, and if she had just accepted that months ago, she might have already started to construct a new life.

Of course, if she had done that, she'd still be sitting here worried that the killer might have found her. Would it have made it any easier for her if she'd allowed herself to put down all those roots she was thinking of now? Not one bit.

In fact, it might have become even scarier. And this was already going to be scary enough.

## Chapter 8

She tried to pass the time reading a book, but that didn't work at all. Wade prowled the house from time to time only to return to the living room and sit for a while. She had no idea if he was peering out windows or what. Maybe he just couldn't hold still.

She could barely stand it herself. Finally she closed the book and looked at him. "Are we supposed to just sit here indefinitely like bumps on a log?"

One corner of Wade's mouth lifted and he came to sit beside her on the sofa. "What would you ordinarily do?"

"Exactly this," she admitted. "Only now I'm too antsy."

"Well, I don't think we should do anything until Gage tells us he has his ducks in a row. Waiting is always the hardest part."

She pursed her lips, trying to find some way to anticipate what might come next. "This guy, this killer, he wasn't afraid to come to our house in the dead of night, knock on the door and shoot everything that moved."

"Apparently not."

"So what's to keep him from doing the same thing here?"

"Nothing, except that I'm an unknown in the equation. That won't hold him back indefinitely, but I'm sure it's giving him pause."

"What kind of pause?"

"He's probably wondering just what kind of protection I can provide. Whether there's a way he can separate us. All of which is based on the assumption that he's really found you."

She sighed. "I wish I knew for certain."

"There are times when you can act, and times when you simply have to *re*act. This is one of those times that we have to wait to react. Because we don't know anything for certain."

She felt a crooked smile twist her lips. "Listen to me. I spent more than a year just letting myself be pushed one way or another and now all of a sudden I want to do something. Anything."

"I know that feeling."

"You probably do." She looked down at the book she was still holding. "I still can't understand what they thought they'd accomplish by killing Jim. It's not like they could erase the grand-jury testimony, or prevent indictments from being handed down."

"I don't know. Maybe they thought that if they removed one prosecutor, the government would have a hard time finding someone else to take over. Intimidation is the only reason I can see."

"I doubt it worked."

"But you don't know?"

She shook her head. "Jim didn't talk about his cases with me. He couldn't. So even if I tried to check newspaper stories or court records, I couldn't tell which case was his."

"But you knew he was after a drug gang."

"That was all I knew. And I'm sure he wasn't the only prosecutor working on a case like that. In a way it's hard not knowing if all his work put those guys in jail. But at the same time…" She shrugged. "What difference does it really make? It won't change anything. Not for me, or Jim, or our baby."

He turned her a little, cupping her chin with his hand, and kissed her gently. "I'm so sorry."

If he meant the kiss to be comforting, it went beyond that. Way beyond that. She wished she knew how his kiss could drive everything else from her mind in a flash. And this one hadn't even attempted to be sexy.

She searched his dark eyes and caught her breath as she saw the heat there. She wasn't alone in her sudden desire, not alone at all. Yet he didn't press her, didn't even try to tip her in that direction.

His hunger for her went straight to her head, lifting her out of herself so that she forgot everything except this man and the heaviness growing between her thighs, a heaviness that demanded an answer.

There was something incredible in arousing a man so powerful and self-contained so easily and quickly. Maybe it was the only way he felt he could truly connect anymore. Maybe he would have responded that way to any woman.

She didn't care. She knew what she wanted, and it was right in front of her. In his eyes she could see that he wanted it, too.

Her fingers moved before she realized it, reaching for

the buttons of his shirt. He waited, letting her unfasten them, watching her face intently the whole time. When the last button was undone, she looked down at this chest and sighed.

"You're beautiful," she said, meaning it. Pressing her palms to that wonderful, warm skin, she ran her hands over him, feeling the rocks and rills of honed muscle, glorying in the sensations and in the way he indulged her exploration.

A slightly ragged breath escaped him. "Are you sure?" he murmured. "Very sure?"

"Yes." The word came out on the last puff of air in her lungs, and hardly had it escaped her, than he scooped her up in his powerful arms and carried her back toward her bedroom.

"I won't stop this time," he warned her. "No half measures."

"I don't want half measures." The truest words she had spoken in a long, long time.

"No quarter," he said.

She wasn't sure what he meant by that, but she was eager to take this ride all the way to the end. Not only did she want this, she needed this. All of it.

He laid her on the bed in her half-darkened room and stood over her like a hero of myth, so big, so hard, almost unreal in his strength and power.

He shrugged off his shirt, then made it clear what was coming when he reached for his belt and the snap of his jeans.

Was she sure? Oh, yes. She watched with hungry fascination, hearing each tooth in the zipper as he drew it slowly down. It was the sexiest sound she had ever heard.

"Stop me now," he said, pausing. "Now."

"No." His own word flung back at him.

She dragged her gaze up from where his hands rested against his fly and saw a lazy smile start to curve his mouth. His eyelids drooped a little with passion, but the rest of his face hardened with hunger.

He kicked off his shoes, then in one smooth movement shoved his pants down and discarded his socks. When he straightened, he was naked to her gaze, and what a breathtaking sight he was.

Michelangelo had never carved a more perfect male body. Nor had anyone to her knowledge ever carved a statue with an erection like that. He was big, he was hard and he was ready.

And the sight of his readiness made her damp, so damp she might have been embarrassed if she weren't already in thrall to her needs. And his. For his need excited her even more than her own.

He bent over her, his fingers pausing just briefly as he once again warned her. "Last chance."

She had begun to pant with the hunger he had already stoked in her, and it was hard to say one word, just one word: "Yesss…"

He stripped her clothes away impatiently, tossing each piece across the room until she lay naked. He paused a moment, drinking her with his eyes, leaving her feeling at once utterly vulnerable and utterly beautiful. No one had ever looked at her like that before, not even Jim, as if she were the most desirable woman he had ever seen. Just that look was enough to make her nipples harden and her center throb so hard it almost hurt.

In that instant, she became woman primal. Everything else vanished entirely. Nothing mattered except this man and this moment. She hardly noticed that he used the few seconds to don protection, because she watched his eyes as they traveled over her like a caress.

Lying over her, his leg pinning hers, his arms holding her tight, he plundered her mouth with a kiss so hungry and needful it echoed all the pain inside her. His hands began to knead her flesh with a heat and longing that just missed being painful. She didn't care. Each touch made her feel so wanted, and oh, heavens, how much she needed to feel wanted.

His mouth closed on her nipple, sending spears of longing straight to her womb. His hand stroked the smooth skin of her hip, and then dived impatiently between her thighs, seeking her heat, her moisture, her life-giving core. She was caught in a storm, with no desire to escape. Whatever he took seemed rightfully his.

Raising his head, he muttered guttural words of encouragement as his touch lifted her higher and higher. Too fast, she thought dizzily, but even that objection drifted away as he took her closer and closer to the brink she dimly sensed was waiting.

"So sweet," he muttered in her ear, and yet another river of excitement poured through her. "Come on, Cory, that's the way."

When her hands clawed at him and the sheets, needing something to hang on to, he grabbed them and moved them upward, wrapping her fingers around the spindles of her headboard. "Hang on," he muttered roughly. "Don't let go." Then he settled between her legs.

Gasping for air, clinging so tightly to the headboard that she dimly felt her hands aching, she opened her eyes and looked up at him. He loomed over her in the dim room, huge and powerful, so strong. She had never imagined, never dreamed, that anything could be as overwhelming as these moments. Every cell in her body was begging for him, begging for completion, for the answer to the screaming ache he had awakened in her body.

He touched her, gently. He found that delicate knot of nerves, then rubbed so carefully, lifting her higher and higher until she hung suspended in exquisite agony and nearly screamed his name.

"Now," he demanded. Slipping an arm beneath her hips, he lifted her to him and took her in one swift, deep thrust, filling an emptiness she had forgotten could exist.

The precipice was close, so close, and his every movement drove her nearer the edge. Letting go of the headboard, she grabbed his shoulders, digging her fingers into smooth, muscled flesh, drawing him down, needing his weight on her as she had seldom needed anything. Needing him.

"Let it happen," he growled in her ear. "Damn it, let it happen!"

Then, with a single, long, deep thrust of his hips, he pushed her over the edge. Moments later his face contorted and he followed her over.

Cory thought the explosion inside her would never end.

They lay tangled together, sweaty and exhausted. Too weary and sated, Cory thought, to work up even a smidgen of fear. The best medicine in the world.

When Wade tried to lever himself off her, she grabbed his shoulders, afraid he might leave.

"I'm not going anywhere," he murmured. He slid off her, to lie beside her on his back, still breathing heavily.

The air felt cool against her hot, damp skin, another delicious contrast. Yes, they needed to cool down, but she hated not feeling the touch of his skin. When she blindly reached out with her hand, his was there to grip hers and hold it. When she gave his fingers a little squeeze, he squeezed back.

"Why can't life always be like this?" she asked softly. As soon as the question emerged, she knew reality was returning, and there was no way to hold it off.

"If life were always like this, we'd never do anything else." He surprised her with a note of humor in his voice.

She turned on her side and smiled at him, a smile that felt easier than any she'd tried to frame in fifteen months. "Would that be so bad?"

A small chuckle escaped him. "No way."

Reaching out, she trailed a finger over his still-damp chest and downward to his hip bone. His manhood responded with a small leap. "Mmm, I could get used to this."

"Used to what?" he asked.

"Having you at my mercy."

"Ah!" In one swift movement, so fast it caught her utterly by surprise, he pushed her on her back and leaned over her, his leg imprisoning hers, his dark eyes holding her. "Who is at whose mercy?"

A truly silly smile rose to her lips. "I like it either way."

"Good." Now he ran a fingertip over her, tracing circles around her breasts and down to her belly, causing her to shiver. "We'll take turns."

"Soon?" she asked hopefully.

"Soon," he said, one corner of his mouth lifting. "But maybe not right now."

She sighed. "Okay."

He lowered his head and brushed a light kiss on her lips. "I'd like nothing better, Cory. But Gage will probably call soon."

She couldn't argue with that, though she wanted to push

back the dark shadows that edged into the corners of her mind. Yes, there were things they had to face, maybe had to face soon, but she felt a huge tide of resentment, something she'd never felt before. Before it had always been the fear and grief, leaving room for little else.

"I resent this," she announced, then instantly regretted her words as she saw him pull back a little. Of course he would misunderstand. "Not you," she hastily said. "I just hate that I'm feeling good for the first time in forever and now I have to think of…of…"

"I understand." His infinitesimal withdrawal vanished as he moved closer, and dropped another light kiss on her mouth.

"How bad was it?" she asked, stroking his short hair as he laid his cheek on her breast.

"What?"

"Your childhood."

He stiffened a bit, and said nothing. Time seemed to drag as she held her breath, wondering if she had pushed too far into tender territory. It really was none of her business, and she suspected this was a man who didn't like admitting his vulnerability, despite what he had tried to share with her over coffee in the wee hours.

"It was bad," he said finally. "I spent a lot of time locked in closets. My dad was fond of whipping me with the buckle end of his belt."

"My God!"

"I survived."

"But…"

He reached up and laid a finger over her mouth. "I survived," he said firmly. "What doesn't kill you makes you stronger."

"You really believe that?"

"Yes."

Perhaps, she thought. Perhaps. But surviving didn't necessarily mean the scars were gone, either emotionally or physically. She had sensed the emotional ones quickly, in some of his almost apologetic statements. As if he felt a need to erase himself. Another thought occurred to her.

"Do you feel like a fish out of water now, away from the SEALs I mean?"

At that he lifted his head. "Lady, if you're going to ask a man to bare his soul, it might be best to let him choose the time and place."

She felt hurt. Unreasonably so, she tried to tell herself, but it didn't quite erase the pang. Logically she knew that women were more likely to become emotionally attached through the act of lovemaking than men, and logically she realized the experience they had just shared had probably made her feel a whole lot closer to him than it had made him feel to her. They were strangers, after all, brought together by a coincidence, and now held together by a threat. He undoubtedly planned to move on as soon as he sorted out whatever it was he had come here to deal with.

And she would be left alone again. Common sense dictated that she not allow herself to grow close to this man. She needed to think of their lovemaking as merely a way to affirm life, and not one thing more.

She ought to know better, and clutching at straws just because a man was decent enough not to leave her in the lurch with this mess was dangerous. She didn't think she could take another loss, so why set herself up for one?

She tried to smile at him, but her face felt pinched. "I need to get dressed. Gage might call at any minute."

"Ah, hell," he said and rolled onto his back.

She looked at him and saw he was staring at the ceiling now. "What?"

"I just hurt you, and I really didn't want to do that."

She felt another pang, this time for him. "No. Really. It's just a girl thing, expecting confidences at a time like this. I know better."

He turned his head to look at her. "I should know better, too. I'm sorry."

Then he jackknifed up off the bed and started hunting up clothes. Hers he dropped beside her on the bed. He climbed into his own swiftly, and left the room before he even finished buttoning and zipping.

One hot tear rolled down Cory's face. She had tried to reach out, and had reached out in exactly the wrong way at the wrong time.

Why would any man want her anyway? She had become a terrified husk of a woman, with nothing left inside her that anyone else would want.

She definitely ought to know better.


Wade stood in the kitchen, filled with self-loathing. He had started another pot of coffee brewing, because coffee had fueled him through some of the most difficult times in his life and had become a habit he clung to the way some people clung to a cup of tea or a blanket for comfort.

He'd drunk it instant, mixed with water barely safe for drinking. He'd sucked it down hot and thick on shipboard. He'd guzzled it thin and watery when what few grounds he had needed to be reused. It didn't much matter how it tasted as much as it mattered that he could cradle a cup in his hands and take comfort in one of life's small habits.

Despite warning himself, he'd taken the step: he'd made love to the woman. And despite warning her and himself that he couldn't make connections, he'd taken the one action most likely to create a connection. You didn't make love to a woman like that and expect her to treat it as a form of entertainment.

So he'd taken that all-too-critical step, he'd started forming a connection, a connection he absolutely believed himself incapable of sustaining. If he had an ounce of common sense, he'd rupture it right now, pack his bags and get out of here before he did some real harm.

He couldn't do that, not with the threat he believed to be lurking. Yes, he knew the sheriff and his entire department would be keeping an eye on Cory. No, he didn't have an inflated sense of his own importance.

But he *did* know how the best net in the world remained a sieve simply because you couldn't plug every hole, and unless Gage meant to assign someone round the clock to stick to Cory's side—and he doubted that because this was a small county and probably had a force just big enough for the ordinary tasks it faced—then someone had to be pinned to Cory's side. Someone who knew how to handle threats like this.

That left him.

Even if others had such training hereabouts, he doubted it was as fresh as his own. He doubted their reflexes remained so honed that the merest glimpse of something moving out of the corner of their eyes could shift them instantly into hyperdrive.

It was true that you never forgot your training, but you could slow down. Hell, hadn't he come here intending to do just that?

So that likely made him the meanest, fastest SOB around here right now. Walking away was not an option.

What to do about Cory? She'd naturally felt their lovemaking had brought them closer, and to be fair, he kind of felt it, too. Not like with the women who'd just wanted to sleep with a SEAL. This was different. Different kind of woman, different kind of experience.

Hell, he wasn't even proud of the way he'd made love to her, so rough and ready, without any of the hearts-and-flowers-type stuff she deserved.

He'd been strung out on need in a way he'd never felt before, and all the self-control he owned seemed to have been focused on giving her a chance to say no. When she hadn't, his self-control had vanished.

And then, after his caveman routine, all she had wanted was to feel closer to him. To know that she hadn't been used like some plastic fantastic lover.

Cripes. He leaned his forehead against the cabinet, waiting for the coffee, and asked himself how he had just managed to mess up two people with one thoughtless act.

But that was him, wasn't it? The whole relationship thing was beyond him, always had been. The relationships he had managed over the years had been built on shared experience and trust within the boundaries of his job. With Cory he had no rules, no guidelines, no purpose other than making sure she survived until they figured out what was going on here.

And he didn't know how to handle it. The only thing he knew for certain was that Cory was as fragile as fine glass emotionally, and he'd probably just added a ding, if not a crack.

He ought to be hanged.

"Wade?"

Her tentative voice reached him from the kitchen entryway. He screwed his eyes shut and tried to get a grip on his self-disgust. "Yeah?"

"I'm sorry. I shouldn't have asked."

He whirled about to find her standing there, clothed

once again, her eyes pinched and lost-looking. She was apologizing when *he'd* put that look back on her face.

"Goddamn it," he said.

Her head jerked. "I'll just leave you alone."

"No."

She hesitated, wrapping her arms around herself as if she needed to hold something in, or hold herself together. "No?" she repeated.

"No. Grab a seat. Stay."

Still she hesitated, but then, after what seemed an eternity, she moved to the table and sat. She kept on hugging herself though, a sure indicator that all was not right in the world of Cory Farland.

He turned his back to her. "I stink at this," he said. Once again he pressed his forehead to the cabinet, glad the coffee hadn't finished yet because it gave him time not to look at her.

"Stink at what?"

"I told you. Connections. Relationships. Whatever the current terminology is. I'm the guy sitting alone at the back of the bar with a beer while the others shoot the breeze. I don't talk about much that isn't mission specific. Nobody really knows me, and I like it that way."

"Because you can't be hurt."

An impatient sound escaped him. "Don't give me the psychobabble. Even if it is true."

"Okay."

The coffee finished, and his excuse was gone. He pulled two mugs from the cupboard and filled them before he carried them to the table. Then he got her milk for her and put it in front of her.

He straddled the chair facing her, but didn't look at her. He didn't want to see that pinched expression again.

"I'm a minefield," he said finally. "Loaded with emotional trip wires. Yeah, I was abused as a kid. So were lots of other people, so don't give me any special passes because of it. I got away as soon as I could, and I promised myself I'd never get into that position again, a position where anyone could beat me up like that. The navy picked me up out of the mud, basically, restored my self-confidence, gave me a purpose and a goal. But they couldn't take away the trip wires. So I learned to keep them buried because they're absolutely useless. What the hell good does it do to keep reacting to things that happened twenty, thirty years ago when they're not still happening?"

She made a little sound but he couldn't tell if she was agreeing.

"What matters," he said finally, "is who I am now. What I became over the years. Unfortunately, I never got around to the part about dealing with people I didn't have a professional relationship with. So I stink at it."

"Mmm." Totally noncommittal. Well, what did he expect when he'd basically told her to shut up while he spewed?

Finally he raised his eyes and looked at her. At least she didn't look ready to shatter any longer. If anything, her face had grown calmer.

"I don't want to talk about when I was a kid," he said. "I don't *need* to talk about it. I got past it the day I realized that if my old man ever came at me like that again I could snap him in two."

She gave a little nod.

"I got past the fear. I got past most of the anger. I got past the feeling of helplessness."

"Good." She lifted her cup and sipped her coffee. "Good."

"Anything that's left is my own fault, not theirs in any way."

"Really."

"Really." And he didn't want to argue about this. "Anything I'm dealing with now is baggage I picked up all on my own."

"Such as?"

"Things I saw, things I did, things I chose not to do. If there's one thing I learned from being in the service, it's that ultimately I'm responsible for myself. The past is past, and it's useless except as a lesson for doing it better next time."

She drew a long breath. "You really believe that?"

"Yes. I do. And I'm quite capable of looking at the things I chose not to do over the years and taking responsibility for them. I chose to let my professional life consume me, I chose not to try to branch out into some kind of normal life. Admittedly, watching my buddies, I eventually concluded it wasn't worth the trouble. At least not while I was still on the job. So it's my fault and nobody else's that I chose not to learn how to build day-to-day relationships apart from the job."

"So you take that whole burden on yourself?"

"Of course. I made the decisions."

"That's a pretty heavy load. Most of us at least accept that our pasts played a role in making us who we are."

"I'm not saying it didn't play a role. But I'm the one, in the end, who says how much and what kind of a role. I'm not arguing that I'm not a product of my past, I'm arguing that I'm a product of the decisions I made in my past."

She nodded slowly, and his gut clenched a bit when he saw her face tightening up. "What?" he asked. "What did I say?"

Her lips tightened. "I'm just thinking about what you said. So you don't even think that as a child you were a victim?"

He shook his head impatiently. "I'm not saying that. When I was a kid, I handled what was dished out to me the best way I could figure out. Every kid does. And when we're kids, we don't have the breadth of experience that comes later, so we're easy to victimize. But later…no. Which is not to say no one is ever a victim. I'm not saying that at all."

"Then what *are* you saying?" she asked, her voice stretched tight.

"I'm saying that it's what we choose to do with it that puts us in control. It's the choices we make, and the lessons we choose to take. And I made some god-awful choices, and maybe I took some of the wrong lessons. That's what I'm saying, and I'm not going to blame any of it on the kid I used to be, because I was a man when I made a lot of these decisions."

She gave a single, jerky nod.

"Cory…what? Am I hurting you? Crap, I don't want to do that."

"No…no. You're making me think."

Oh, hell. He suddenly realized how she could be taking this. "I'm not criticizing *you*. I'm not saying you weren't a victim."

"I know that. I get that. It's just that…"

He waited, and when she didn't speak, he finally prodded. "Just that what?"

"Just that you're right. I've kind of been thinking along the same lines over the past couple of days. That bastard stole my husband, my baby, my old life. But I'm still breathing. So what did I do? I crawled into a hole in the ground and stopped living. I chose to let him take away even my hope."

"Aw, hell." He couldn't take any more of this. He rose from the table, knocking over the chair and ignoring it. He rounded to her and scooped her right up out of her chair, carrying her to the living room where he sat with her in his lap.

"You don't get it," he whispered, hugging her close. "You didn't do anything wrong. Everyone needs time to heal before they can get going again. You needed the time. You *needed* it. I keep telling you that. What if you'd had your leg blown off? Do you think you could skip surgery and rehab? Of course not. All I'm trying to tell you is that I take responsibility for the fact that I chose not to learn basic life skills. Like how to talk to a lady. Like how to reach out. Like how to share myself."

"Actually," she said brokenly, "I think you're doing a damn fine job of it right now."

"Not good enough. I've hurt you twice in the past half hour. I'm ham-fisted at this."

Her hand gripped his shirt, balling it. "Listen to yourself. Just listen. You'll make all kinds of excuses for me, but none for yourself. Think about that, Wade. The people who used to beat you up are gone from your life. So what do you do? You beat yourself up *for* them."

He grew so still and silent that she almost panicked. Had she done it again? Pushed him to places he was unwilling to go, to even look at? She tensed herself, in expectation that he'd toss her off his lap and walk out the door never to be seen again.

But then, finally, she felt him relax. His hand covered hers, where it knotted his shirt, and held it.

"Maybe you're right," he said gruffly.

"Maybe you think you can't make connections, but have you ever tried? You're doing just fine with me."

"But I hurt you."

"So? That's part of any relationship. People hurt each

other. When it's unintentional, it's okay. I don't think you want to hurt me. Do you?"

"Hell no."

"Then okay. It happens." She sighed. "Do you think my marriage to Jim was pure perfection? We had our fights. We hurt each other sometimes. The important thing is forgiving and forgetting when the hurt wasn't intentional. *That's* how you make a relationship that works."

He turned that around in his mind, giving her credit for being far more adult in some ways than he was. "With me a person would need the patience of a saint."

"Same here." She squirmed a little on his lap, reminding him that he still wanted her like hell on fire, then rested her head against his shoulder. "We've all got trip wires, Wade. Fact of life. And when those wires get laid by terrible emotional experiences, they're hard to get rid of."

"Well, I laid a lot more of them over the years." He didn't have to look very far back to see where they'd come from. "Combat vets get lots of them. A sound. A sight. A smell. Even a word. I told you I can't hold still. That's not purely my training at work. It's my learning."

"Learning?"

"How long do you think you can live on the edge before living on the edge becomes the only way to live? You think you can unwind just because you're home, out of the zone? Too many of us drink too much because it's the only way to wind down. Others of us just live with the constant skin-crawling feeling that something is about to happen, that we can't relax for even a minute."

She nodded against his shoulder, just a small movement. "I've lived that way for a little over a year. You've lived that way your whole life. Insecure, sure something bad is always just around the corner."

"Yeah. It makes me explosive, like a bomb." He sighed,

not sure where he wanted to take this, not sure why he was spilling his guts like this. Maybe he was hoping that his warning would get through, that she'd back away. Or maybe he was hoping that the next time he did or said something wrong she'd understand he didn't mean to hurt her.

But regardless of what she understood, he would hurt her. He'd slam an emotional door in her face, or retreat behind his personal drawbridge. In one way or another, he'd go into self-protection mode, and once he got into that mode, he might well stage a preemptive attack.

"You've got to understand," he said roughly. "You have to."

"Understand what?"

"That protecting myself is automatic. Regardless of the kind of threat."

She tipped her head against his shoulder and he knew she was looking up at him. He refused to look back at her. Let her read what she could from his chin; he wouldn't give her any more than that. Not right now. Maybe never.

"Okay," she said finally. "You protect yourself. I understand that."

A frustrated sound escaped him. "Do you understand what that might mean?"

"Maybe not in every detail. But I get the general picture."

He envied the note of confidence in her voice, but he didn't believe it. Whatever this woman had been through in her life, and the little she had told him had been bad enough, he didn't think it could possibly prepare her for what he could dish out. She had absolutely no idea of all that he was capable of.

But he did. That was the curse of so many years in Special ops. You knew what your limits were, and worse, you discovered you didn't have a whole lot of them. Whatever the mission required. And sometimes the mission was your own self-protection.

That didn't mean he was ashamed of himself, because he wasn't. But it did mean he knew himself in ways most people never faced. Most people never needed to look into the darkest parts of human nature. And people like him were the reason they never had to. But those who had looked…well, they lived in an uncomfortable world with all the rosy tint stripped away.

It was a sad fact of life that someone needed to visit those black places, that someone needed to come face-to-face with the ugliest things in the human heart and soul.

But those who went there remained apart and different because once you'd looked into the abyss, it became part of you.

She thought she understood, God bless her. She thought because she had seen the terrible thing the night the killer came to her house, that she had some idea. But she had no idea at all, because seeing was not the same as doing. Sometimes a person like Cory glimpsed the abyss. But folks like him not only glimpsed it. They walked into it. They melded with it.

And when they returned they were forever changed in ways only someone who had trod the path with them could imagine.

So how the hell did you get around that?

# Chapter 9

Gage called during the early afternoon. Cory got the cordless-extension phone from her bedroom so they could both listen to him and talk as necessary.

"Okay," Gage said. "I've got both pictures going out to all deputies. They're not being told anything about you, Cory, just that I want these guys hauled in on sight for questioning in a possible homicide case. They're to be treated as armed and dangerous."

Cory caught her breath inaudibly at the description, then wondered why. It wasn't as if she didn't already know how dangerous these guys were. But somehow hearing it from Gage's lips made the threat seem more imminent. He had removed it from the realm of speculation and put it out there as reality.

Only as she felt her heart slam in response did she realize just how much denial she had been living with. Yes, she'd been afraid, maybe even ridiculously afraid all this time, but at some level she had desperately believed this moment would never come. And even now a part of her brain insisted on saying, *We don't know for sure*.

And that was true. They were acting on little more than suspicion and a confluence of coincidences. As Jim had so often said of such things, "It won't stand up in court."

Gage knew that, surely. Yet he was moving forward as if a real threat had been made.

And maybe it had, in that phone call. It had certainly been made a year ago when the Marshals decided they had to put her into permanent protection. After all, it wasn't as if they were manufacturing a paranoid conspiracy out of whole cloth.

She barely listened to the discussion the two men were having. It was as if a switch had been thrown at the instant she had faced the naked threat yet again. Once again she felt numb, utterly numb, perhaps even hollow. Yet there seemed to be no place left inside her for the fear, or even anger. In fact, even the spark of hope that had ignited in her over the past couple of days had deserted her.

There was nothing, could *be* nothing for her ever, unless she got this threat off her back for good.

Sitting there, hardly hearing as the two men talked, she faced the dismal reality of what her life had become and what it would remain as long as that killer was after her.

There would be no recovery, no hope, no future. That was what that man and his vendetta had done to her. He might as well have finished her off with a bullet to the head.

She couldn't go back to the woman she had been just a few days ago. Because over the past few days, she had tasted hope and life again, however briefly. She might have found just the illusion of it in Wade's arms, but it was enough to make her realize she could not go back. Whatever the cost.

Into the emptiness crept a steely resolve unlike anything she had ever felt before. Death, she knew in her heart, was infinitely preferable to the way she had been existing. She could not, would not, go back to that.

Nor did she pin her hopes for a future on Wade. She understood that he was a troubled, complex, complicated man who had come here seeking some kind of release, but he would have to find that on his own. Just as she would have to find her own resolve to live again, for *herself*.

No crutches, for they were unreliable, and temporary at best. So, she thought, as ice seemed to settle over her, she would deal with this mess. Then she would look for the woman she wanted to become. The woman who had once loved being a teacher. The woman who had enjoyed cooking as if her own kitchen was part of the finest restaurant.

And perhaps she'd discover other parts of herself in the process, parts she'd never had a chance to find before because she'd been too preoccupied with her goals, and then with Jim.

She was, she resolved, going to find her own two feet.

And the first step was getting rid of this threat. Allowing it to steal not one more day of her life.

She hung up the phone before the two men even finished their conversation. The details of what they planned really didn't matter.

All that mattered was that she was going to face down her husband's killer or die trying.

It didn't take Wade long to notice the change in her. She sensed him start watching her more closely a couple of hours later. She didn't care. He could watch her all he wanted. If she'd had a psychological break of some kind, it was a beneficial one.

She had had enough.

If that meant turning into an ice queen until this was over, then that was fine by her. Remembering how she had collapsed only two days ago after that phone call, she looked at herself and decided ice was infinitely preferable to that. Death was infinitely preferable to that. She had paid the price for someone else's criminal act long enough.

She started dinner at her usual time. Wade joined her, but didn't say anything. Nor did she have much to say, except to give him directions, since he seemed determined to help. Nothing personal. Nothing emotive. Just dry, flat instructions.

She felt no particular desire to eat, recognizing her hunger only as a sign she needed fuel. She didn't even allow herself to enjoy the tasks in the kitchen. Not now. No way.

Not even in the littlest way did she want to feel regret for what was gone. No room for that now.

Finally, over dinner, he asked, "What's going on?"

"What do you mean?"

"You've got a thousand-yard stare."

That at least caught her interest. "What's that?"

"It's the way men look coming out of battle. Distant. Shut down."

She forked some salad and ate it, pondering the comment as an intellectual exercise, having no other reaction to it. "I guess that would about cover it," she finally said.

"Did something happen?"

She barely glanced at him. "I've had enough. That's all. This gets finished if I have to hunt that man myself."

"I see."

He probably did. She returned to eating.

He resumed eating, too. But after a few minutes he spoke. "I get worried when I see that look."

"Oh? Why?"

"Because when I see it, it means someone really *has* had enough. That the only way they can keep from breaking is to totally withdraw. It's usually a sign of post-traumatic stress disorder."

"Hmm. Well, I probably have that, too."

"Probably."

Again silence fell. Then, "Cory?"

"What?"

"It's not good."

She raised her gaze from her plate. "What's not good? That I've decided enough is enough? That I've decided I'm going to get my life back or die trying?"

He shook his head. "That's not what I mean."

"Then what do you mean?"

"Shutting down. Not caring. That's dangerous. I've seen men do stupid things and get themselves killed when they have that look in their eyes."

She simply looked at him, then resumed eating. Go back to what she had felt before? No way. This was infinitely preferable to feeling.

Wade didn't say any more as they finished the meal. She barely tasted it. Fuel, nothing more. He joined her in the washing up, so it didn't take long.

Then there was nothing to do except wait. The thing was, she didn't want to wait. Not anymore. The Sword of Damocles no longer frightened her, but it was still hanging over her head.

"I'm going to take a walk," she announced.

"Not without me."

"I didn't say I was going alone."

"Okay," he said. "Okay."

\* \* \*

Oh, he didn't like that look in her eyes at all. He pulled on his boots, lacing them tightly, readying himself. He even went so far as to put his sheathed knife on his belt, then let his shirttails hang out over it. He could throw that knife with as much accuracy over short distances as he could hit a target with a gun from seven hundred yards. These were some of the skills he'd learned, used and had to live with.

And since he couldn't carry a rifle with him on the streets, the knife would have to do. As would the garrote he stuck into his pocket, and the three plastic ties that could double as handcuffs.

Even if he went to prison for the rest of his life for it, he would allow nothing to harm Cory. Nothing. The certainty settled into his heart with entirely too much familiarity. It was not a new feeling, and he knew to the nth degree what he could do when he felt like this.

He supposed he was now wearing his own thousand-yard stare. The calm of imminent battle had settled over him.

The feeling was as familiar as a well-broken pair of boots, like those he had just donned. Comfortable, but that didn't mean he liked it. He'd been in enough battles to know better. Even success seldom left a good taste in his mouth. Or a totally quiet conscience.

Even less did he like the way the skin on the back of his neck crawled. It was back, all of it, just like that: everything he'd tried to shed and untangle over the past six months resurrected as if it had never gone away.

The man he wanted to leave behind took over now, emerging front and center almost mockingly. It didn't matter, though. This was the man he had chosen to become over many years, and now he needed to be that man again. For Cory's sake.

Whatever it took. Mission-specific goals became paramount, pushing everything else into the background. The man he had hoped he might become would just have to wait for another day.

Even in battle mode, however, he wished Cory wouldn't take this walk. It would create unnecessary, uncontrolled exposure. Things like this should be planned in advance, contingencies reviewed.

But much as he wished she wouldn't do this, he could see that nothing was going to stop her short of breaking the law and keeping her a prisoner in her own home. As he had said, when he saw that look in someone's eye, he knew they were capable of doing something stupid.

All he could do was call Gage and tell him what he and Cory were about to do.

"Are you out of your minds?" Gage asked.

"I can't stop her short of imprisoning her. You want to come argue?"

"Hell. All right, I'll see if I can get some people in the vicinity fast."

After he hung up the phone, he went to meet Cory at the front door. Her eyes remained flat and empty, but her body was moving impatiently. God, he knew that feeling all too well.

"I can't talk you out of this?" he asked quietly.

She just looked at him and switched off the alarm. He was the one who had to punch it to reset it before they slipped out the door.

This was definitely not good.

She paused on the front porch as if deciding which direction to take.

"You need to think," he said.

"I *am* thinking."

"No, you're trying to take the bull by the horns without any adequate preparation. You should stay inside and let me scout first."

"I want my life back. And I'm through waiting for that bastard to give it back."

He could understand that. He could even identify with it. What worried him was the flatness of her statement. If she'd been angry or upset, he'd have had a chance to reason with her. But in this state, there would be no reasoning.

She turned away from the park. He took it as a good sign. She might be utterly reckless with her own safety, but not even in her present mood was she prepared to risk the families and children who might be in the park.

She walked briskly, as if she had somewhere to go. That was fine by him. His own senses went on high alert, his field of vision widening as he slipped into the mode where his brain paid as much attention to his peripheral vision as to his central field. Maybe more. For most people that happened only with an adrenaline rush. For him it happened from long practice.

The same thing with his hearing. The brain usually filtered most sounds, prioritizing and even making people unaware of background noise at a conscious level. But like a person who'd been hard of hearing for a while and had just gotten his first hearing aid, when he went into this mode every sound became equally important, and none were dismissed as mere distraction.

Hyperaware, hyperalert. All without a whisper of adrenaline. Unfortunately, Cory had none of his training, and in her current state, she most likely wouldn't have adrenaline to sharpen her senses.

Which made her a liability.

Cripes, he hoped she walked off this mood. It wasn't

that he wanted her to be terrified, but a reasonable caution would be nice. A person couldn't make good decisions without even a modicum of fear in a dangerous situation.

Which was what he had been trying to tell her a little while ago. And she just plain wasn't listening.

Well, it wasn't as if he hadn't seen this before. Hadn't dealt with it before. It could happen to a man at any time: after his first battle, after a particularly nasty or long-lasting fight, or for no discernible reason at all. It just happened. Some cog slipped and everything shut down.

He supposed it was a form of self-protection and probably had its uses as long as it didn't go on too long, or start happening inappropriately.

They took a power walk, as he'd heard some describe it. Not quite running or jogging, but it would have been impossible to move any faster and still call it walking. When he glanced at Cory, he saw her face was still set in a blank expression, and perspiration had begun to give her skin a dewy look.

But he didn't look at her often. With his senses stretched he was trying to take in and process every sight, sound and smell within reach.

And he memorized the layout of the area for several miles around Cory's house. It pleased him about as much as the mountains of Afghanistan had. This might not be mountains with boulders and caves to hide behind at every turn, but the houses, garages, cars, trees and shrubs served the same purpose, and like many older towns, the houses nearly hugged each other. The people who had originally built this area had been looking for comfort in numbers, not privacy by lawns.

He wondered if she had any idea that pacing up and down every street as she did was a good recon. Probably not. Such things were undoubtedly far from her mind.

And as they walked, he noticed an increasing number of patrol cars. Nothing truly obvious, but probably more of a show of force than this neighborhood routinely saw.

He honestly didn't know if that was good. Scaring these guys off temporarily would only delay the problem. But one thing he was sure of by the time they marched back up onto Cory's porch was that he'd caught no sight of the man, or either of his cars, that had set off his internal alarms.

What did that mean? He could think of answers both good and bad.

Inside the house, once he reset the alarm, he watched Cory march down the hallway to her bedroom, then he heard her shower come on.

Damn, this house was stuffy. It held the day's warmth close, and the smells of their meal still filled the air. Imagine having lived like this for the past year, afraid to even open a window.

On impulse, he switched off the alarm, and opened a window in the living room, and another in her kitchen, allowing the freshening evening breeze to blow through. He could keep an eye on both while she showered, and the breeze would clear out the downstairs in only a few minutes.

Then it occurred to him that by shutting down the alarm system, he had left every window in the house unprotected against intrusion.

Well, hell. Sighing impatiently, he went back to the keypad and looked through all the warnings it gave him and finally got to the question about bypassing zones. He hesitated only a moment, taking time to scan the list of zones on the plastic card behind the keypad. Okay. He could switch off the living room and kitchen, and leave the rest of the house online.

He hit the bypass for each zone, then re-enabled the

alarm. Now all he had to do was keep an eye out and wait to see what emerged from the shower. A woman who had collected herself, or one who remained withdrawn.

She did emerge finally, wearing a scanty tank top and shorts. He spared a moment to notice those lovely legs and graceful arms. She seemed not to notice he had opened the windows, nor to care, although she probably would shortly. The dry air held heat poorly, and as the sun sank the breeze had just begun to take on a chill.

Cory seemed oblivious, however, going to the living room and sitting on the couch, staring at nothing in particular.

He decided he needed to try to engage her again. Try to draw her out of that netherworld where the brain and emotions went when they felt overwhelmed.

"Cory?"

She barely glanced at him.

"What happened?"

"What *do* you mean?"

At least she was answering him. "I mean what made you…" He hesitated, not wanting to use the word *snap*. A person in this state could switch from withdrawal to rage in an instant. "What pushed you over the edge?" he said finally, realizing there was no delicate way to phrase this.

"All of it."

"Well, yes." This was like walking through a minefield. "But something particular happened to put that look in your eye."

The slightest movement of her shoulder suggested a shrug. "You and Gage were talking on the phone. That's when I realized that I don't want to live this way anymore. I refuse to live this way any longer. I'm done with it."

Good. She was talking. "That's understandable."

"There's no point in living if I have to live this way. So I just won't do it anymore."

And that was where the danger lay. That came awfully close to suicidal thoughts. He sought a way to get through the cloak of detachment that shrouded her. "Making up your mind that you've had enough shouldn't lead you to act rashly."

"Why not?" Her hollow eyes regarded him unblinkingly. "Why should I put up with this one day, one hour, longer than necessary?"

"Because once we deal with this, it would be nice for you to be around to try building a new life."

"What am I supposed to build a new life with? That bastard took everything that mattered to me, directly or indirectly. Survival is not enough."

"Then what is?"

Finally he saw a spark of life in her gaze. Just a spark. "I don't know. I don't care anymore."

"Yes, you do."

She looked away, saying nothing.

"Admit it, Cory. In the past couple of days you've started to feel a little hope again. A little pleasure. You've tasted the idea that life could be good again."

"No." She turned to face him, and now she was angry. Good and angry. Part of the reaction, but in its own way as difficult to deal with as the distancing.

"Do you really think," she said, "that sex with you is enough to make life good again? Do you really think a hasty tumble in the hay is all I need to make things better? God, even a man should know better than that."

He didn't argue. She was right. Even if it stung.

"For the love of heaven," she said, jumping to her feet. "I'm living in a prison! I got a couple of hours of parole but that's all I got. And then I asked myself why I should start hoping again. What makes me think this mess is going to get any better? That there'll be anything left for me except ashes even if we do catch this guy."

She rounded on him. "The Marshals haven't caught him in all these months. Fifteen months the Marshals and FBI have been hunting this man and they can't find him. In fact, I bet if I checked with them, I'd find out he's moved down their priority list to a level below some escaped felon or some bank robber. Just another ice-cold case."

He remained silent, letting her rant however she needed to.

"If they ever find this guy, it's going to be because he comes after me. And now you and Gage even suspect that somebody must have revealed my location. Some protection. All they did was take away the little I had left. They should have just let me go home to my blood-soaked condo. At least I wouldn't have had to endure a year of this!"

She wrapped her arms around herself and began pacing the small living room. "What they did was put me in solitary confinement. You say you can't make connections? I haven't been able to because getting too close to someone increased the possibility that I'd say something I shouldn't. Look at how fast you picked up on it from things I didn't say. They told me I'd be safe once they moved me, but I never believed it. How could I believe it when they couldn't catch the gunman and I was the only one who could identify him? How could I believe it when that monster who killed my husband put a contract on me?"

"I don't know," he said quietly, mostly to show that he was listening.

"You know what I think?" she demanded.

"No."

"I think they put me into Witness Protection because I

was an ongoing embarrassment. They couldn't catch the bad guy, they couldn't send me back to my life for fear I'd become a front-page scandal if I turned up dead. So they sent me away. Far away. And once they got me settled in this rundown house with a minimum-wage job, they handed me a couple of business cards and never looked back. Problem solved."

"You believe that?"

"What else am I supposed to believe? Here I am, a year after they dumped me, and that killer may be after me because of them. He may have found me because of them."

"We don't know that."

"How else would he have found me here? Look around you, Wade. Does this look like the kind of place you try to hide a witness? Newcomers here stick out. So why the hell did they pick this place? Why not some major city where I'd be just one of millions?"

It was a good question and had already occurred to him. "Maybe they thought no one would ever look in a place like this."

"Clearly they may have been wrong. Regardless, here I am, all alone, facing the thing they said they were protecting me from."

He lowered his voice even more. "You're not alone."

"Not now. Because you just happened to land here looking for peace. Bet they didn't count on that."

Uneasiness began to creep through him. "Do you know what you're saying?"

"Yes!"

"There's just one problem with that. A phone call."

She threw up a hand. "So? Like you said, the guy needed to figure out which of a number of women who moved here in the last year was the right one. But if you're at all right about that call, and that guy we ran into, someone put him on my tail. And the only people aside from Gage who are supposed to know where I am are the Marshals."

He didn't speak, just turned her paranoia around in his mind, testing it for validity.

"I mean, how am I supposed to know that Seth Hardin sent you here? Because Gage said so? Because Gage said you've got a wall full of medals and you check out? That doesn't mean you didn't come here for some other purpose. I can't even trust you. You're a trained killer yourself and you figured out my situation pretty darn fast."

At that, everything inside him went still, cold and silent. Everything she said was true, insofar as it went. But it was twisted through the lens of fear and paranoia and trauma. Regardless, he never again was going to let anyone kick him this way. Bad enough he had to live with what he was, without someone using it against him to claim he was untrustworthy.

He stood. "I'll leave."

She didn't answer, just continued to stand there hugging herself and glaring.

"But let me make one thing clear to you, lady. I don't lie, and good men in far worse situations than this have trusted me. I never betray a trust."

He turned, then remembered the windows. Without a word, he slammed the living room window shut and locked it. Then he went to do the same in the kitchen and came back to reset the alarm. Cory suddenly appeared beside him.

"I'll be gone in less than thirty minutes," he said tautly.

"Wade…"

"No, Cory. Not another word. Nobody talks to me that way."

He was halfway up the stairs when he heard her start sobbing.

# *Chapter 10*

Oh, God, what had she done? The numbness that had sheltered her most of the afternoon and evening had vanished, first leaving her furious, then filling her with despair as she heard her own words about Wade play back in her mind.

As she started sobbing, he just kept climbing the stairs, never looking back. And she couldn't blame him, she could only blame herself. Where had that ugliness come from, all that suspicion? How could such words have passed her lips? How could such thoughts have entered her mind, especially when she knew something of Wade's background.

It was as if an evil genie had taken over her tongue, spewing vile words as if they had some basis in truth.

But they had none. Only moments after having said those things, she had realized she didn't believe them. Not about Wade. And now she couldn't call those words back.

She returned to the living room and curled up in a ball on the couch, letting the tears flow. Facing the fact that she had become some kind of emotional cripple. Nothing worked right anymore. Nothing. Her whole psyche was so messed up that the normalcy she'd been pining for over the past few days would probably escape her forever.

If she survived this. And the really scary thing was that she didn't even care anymore if she did. She just wanted to be done with it.

So what had she done? She'd struck out at the one person who had managed to make her want to live again. That was the real threat he posed: that he had made her want to move past this nightmare into a future of some kind. That he had made her want to start looking forward again, rather than back.

And she had struck at him in the way she had guessed would hurt him the most: attacking his honor.

What kind of person had she become? She didn't like herself at all anymore, not one little bit. Turning over, she buried her face in a throw pillow and wondered if she'd ever again be able to justify the space she took up on this planet. Because right now she had to face the fact she was a waste of life. A mean waste of life.

These weren't the lessons she should take from what had happened to her. My God, she'd been a teacher. How many times had she tried to help students learn to grow from their bad experiences? How many times had she painted object lessons in how even a bad experience could be turned to something good?

Now look at her. She couldn't even take her own advice.

Finally the tears stopped, simply because there were none left. The storm had moved through, but this time it hadn't left her feeling totally numb. No, she still hurt, and she despised herself. No convenient, comfortable numbness now.

She sat up finally to find the house dark. Even more surprising, however, was that she saw Wade sitting in the recliner across from her, a bulky shadow among shadows.

"I thought you were leaving."

"I don't abandon my post."

Totally neutral. As if he had put his own feelings away in a vault somewhere, as she had for hours today.

"I'm sorry," she said. "I can't tell you how sorry. I don't know where that ugliness came from."

"Doesn't matter." Indifferent. Unrevealing. The way he had seemed when he first arrived.

She had done that, she admitted. She had driven him back into that place where the walls were high and the battlements well guarded. And there was no way she could call back those words. "I'm sorry," she said again, useless words once the wounds had been inflicted. "I didn't even mean it. I don't know what I was thinking."

"You weren't thinking."

"Obviously. I was acting like an animal, striking out at everything indiscriminately."

"Maybe so."

Oh, he was giving her nothing, not one little thing. Could she blame him? "I was afraid."

"No, you were angry."

"They come from the same thing."

"Mmm."

God, it was like talking to a brick wall again. And now it was not just annoying or disturbing. Now it hurt. It was almost enough to make her mad again, that he could hurt her this way.

She sat silently for a while, scrubbing the dried tears

from her face. Finally she decided the only way to get past his walls was to lower her own. Her heart accelerated a bit at the danger in exposing herself this way. But she owed it to him, especially since after what she had said he was still in this house, still ready to protect her even with his life. Didn't such a man deserve the truth?

"I was…I was striking out because you made me start to hope again. I was afraid because you made me feel that a normal life might be possible for me. And I don't believe that anymore. I can't believe that. Look at me. I'm damaged goods. I'll never be normal again."

"It's unlikely."

Damn! She couldn't believe she had done this to him, and it was too late to rip out her own tongue.

Then, finally, in the dark so she couldn't even attempt to read his face, he began to speak. His tone was measured, his words slow.

"Nobody," he said, "who has seen and experienced what you and I have seen and experienced will ever be so-called normal again. It's an impossible thing to ask."

"I guess so." A hot, stray tear trickled down her cheek and she dashed it away.

"There will always be scars," he continued. "Things will never look the way they used to before violence entered our lives."

"No." Now she sounded like him.

A few seconds ticked by. Then, "But just because we carry scars, just because we've lived through things a lot of other people don't, doesn't mean there's anything wrong with us. Far too many people in this world have experienced violence in one form or another. Maybe that makes us more normal than those who haven't."

"What an awful thought." One that caused her a pang, not only for all the others of whom he spoke, but because it reminded her just how much self-pity she'd indulged, maybe was still indulging. He was right, and she knew it. One only had to turn on the news to see what millions of others suffered, many on a daily basis.

"Maybe. Still true. I've seen a lot of the world, and violence touches more lives than you can imagine. I'm not saying that's right, I'm just saying it is."

"You're right." Her voice broke a little. "I was protected from it all my life."

"Some people are. Some of us are lucky enough not to live in war zones, or among thugs. But an awful lot of us, sooner or later, taste the ugliest side of human nature. Unfortunately, you didn't even have a support group of friends and family who shared your experience. Maybe that's the worst thing WITSEC did to you. It protected you physically, but left you with no help to heal emotionally."

She caught her breath. "Maybe," she agreed.

"Most of us are luckier than you. We have all kinds of social support."

"You didn't, when you were a child."

"No, but I sure as hell did after I grew up. But the scars are still there. All of them. Unlike you, I've had decades to deal with my crap. You haven't. And you can see what a stellar example of healing I am."

"Don't knock yourself. I already did that, and unfairly, too."

"I'm just trying to make a point. You *can* have a life again. It's just that sometimes you're going to hurt. Always."

"I guess so."

"With time the hurting comes less often. But it never entirely vanishes. Sorry, but I can't offer more than that."

"It should be enough."

"It's life. Whether it's enough is something only you can decide."

"I'd almost decided. Then…well, you saw what happened."

"Yeah." He was silent a moment, then with a surprising note of humor he added, "You tried to build your walls back up with dynamite."

She winced, because the description was so apt. And the only person who'd been hurt by her explosion was him. She'd had no idea she could turn so ugly, and the knowledge didn't comfort her at all. "My explosion didn't work very well. I'm sorry."

"It's okay," he said finally. "I understand, believe me. I've seen it plenty of times, even done it myself a few times. That's what I meant about trip wires. You just start thinking you might reach for the brass ring, and then everything inside you starts shrieking warnings. Hell, you probably don't even believe you're entitled to live a normal life."

She honestly hadn't looked at it that way before, but the sinking in her stomach acknowledged the truth of his words. "That's a place I haven't gone."

"Not yet, maybe. You will. At some point, if it hasn't already, survivor guilt will give you a rough ride. If it does, and I'm around, talk to me about it. Been there, done that."

*If* he was around. That word caused her another sharp pang. "God, I'm a mess."

"No more so than anyone else in your shoes. Try to find some comfort in that."

"I can't believe you're trying to make me feel better after the way I treated you. You're being awfully generous." And that made him a truly remarkable person, in anyone's book.

"Don't beat yourself up." His tone had grown softer,

kinder than when they had begun this conversation, and that only made her feel worse.

"But the things I said!"

"I don't blame you for them. After I got upstairs and cooled off a bit, I realized you touched one of my trip wires. At least one. I overreacted."

"I don't think you did." She was still aching over the things she had said and implied about him. "You offered to protect me when you didn't need to do a thing. You deserve better from me."

"You didn't say anything so god-awful, in the circumstances. Just let it go. I have."

But had he? He might say so, but given the way he had responded, she knew full well her angry words must have cut him to the quick in the places that mattered most to him, like his sense of duty and honor. Ideals to which he'd devoted his entire adult life. Maybe he wasn't proud of everything he'd had to do. She could scarcely imagine the kinds of jobs SEALs must be sent on. Maybe some of those things even stuck in his craw. But she was fairly certain he'd never betrayed one of his buddies, and had never failed in his duty. And she'd made him sound like nothing better than a hired gun.

God, she wished she could erase the memory of her words.

"Ah, damn, lady," he said on a sigh, "just let it go. Don't you think you already have enough baggage?"

"Maybe, but that doesn't give me the right to hand out more of it to anyone."

"You didn't hand me any baggage. Period."

Of course not. She didn't matter enough to him to be able to hurt him that way. In one sense she felt relieved that her shrewing hadn't hurt him in any lasting way. In another, awfully selfish way, she didn't like that she mattered so little to him. But why should she? Two days did not a relationship make. Not even good sex could make up for lack of time.

And, as he had told her more than once, he didn't make those kinds of connections anyway. So maybe she shouldn't feel bad about what she had said, at least as far as hurting him went. He didn't allow himself that kind of vulnerability.

Judging by the way he had initially reacted to her rant, she supposed he wasn't totally impervious. At least not at that moment in time, although she would guess she had sent him back to that place where he let nothing touch him.

But there was more at issue here than whether she had hurt him. She had behaved deplorably, according to her own standards whether she had wounded him or not.

He surprised her then by rising and crossing the room to stand in front of her. It was still dark, the room illuminated only by the faintest light from outside streetlamps that managed to creep around cracks in the corner.

"I want you," he said baldly.

Her heart leaped instantly. Something about her loved the way he was so open and honest about his needs, the way he voiced them without varnish or hesitation. Best of all, without embarrassment. That freed her from all those things, too.

She lifted a hand to take his. "Just don't carry me."

"Why not?"

"Because just once I'd like to get into bed with you under my own steam."

At that he laughed. "It's a deal. Sorry, I guess I've been picking you up a lot."

"Only a few times." She answered the gentle tug of his hand and rose to her feet. "Why do you do that?"

"I don't know." He said nothing for a few seconds, still

holding her hand. "Maybe," he said finally, almost breaking her heart in the process, "it's the only way I know to keep you close."

Ah, God, that was such a revealing thing for him to say, as if he had stripped his mind and emotions bare. It was one thing to say you wanted someone sexually. It was entirely another to admit you wanted to keep them close but didn't know how. Her throat tightened so that she couldn't even speak.

All she could do was stare starkly at the fact that they were both wounded souls, each in their own broken way trying to make some kind of connection again, regardless of what either of them might claim. He sought physical connections because he didn't know how to make the other kind. She fought emotional connections because they hurt too much, and found the same solace he did in the physical.

Was that wrong? No, it wasn't. And maybe it was the first step on a much longer path they both needed to walk, whether together or separately. She squeezed his fingers to show her understanding, then cleared her throat, finding her voice again.

"I, um, guess it's okay if you carry me then."

A little laugh escaped him. "Oddly, I think I'd prefer it a whole lot more if you came with me, Cory. Come lie with me, lady."

He couldn't have chosen words more likely to ignite her desire, though she couldn't have said why. Heat spiraled through her to her very core, making her feel heavy with longing. Already her body ached for his touches, for his weight, for the fullness of feeling him inside her. She'd felt desire before in her life, but never this hot and this fast.

And he did that with simple words. Somehow that *come lie with me* affected her more viscerally than, *let's make love,* or many of the other affectionate or teasing suggestions she used to hear from Jim. *Come lie with me.*

The words made her nerves hum, and she had no desire to analyze any further. She was tired of being under a microscope, his or her own. Wade offered her the freedom to be, just be, in this moment and no other. And she reached out with both hands for the gift.

This time he evidently felt no desire for the rough-and-ready matings they'd had before. This time he stood beside the bed with her, and began to remove her clothing slowly, almost as if he were unwrapping a present and wanted to savor the anticipation a little longer. To draw out each moment of expectation.

He took his time even with things that should have happened quickly, like lifting her tank top over her head. Trailing his fingers up her sides as he did so sent ripples of longing through her for more. Oh, she felt so greedy, and he made her feel that way.

Then he followed the movement all the way up as he lifted the top, tracing the most sensitive parts of her inner arms all the way to her fingertips. When he at last tossed the top aside, she felt almost worshipped.

Nor did he stop there. He cast aside his own shirt, and the darkness in the room added to the mystery of all that was happening inside her. When his hands gently gripped her waist and pulled her close, there was something inexplicably exquisite about the feeling of his skin against her belly, except for her breasts, still shrouded by her bra. Then he bent and took her mouth in a kiss that stole her breath, and seemed to touch her very soul. His tongue mated slowly with hers as his fingertips drew gentle patterns on her back and sides, promising so much, taking nothing at all. He merely ignited her cells one by one until she felt alive with fire.

Then his mouth left hers, trailing slowly down her neck, causing her to arch and moan softly with delight.

"You are so sexy," he murmured against her neck, his breath hot and moist. A shiver rippled through her. Had anything ever felt this exquisite?

On a wisp of breath she answered, "You make me feel so sexy."

"Good. Good." His mouth trailed lower, lips and tongue outlining the cups of her bra, promising but not giving. Not yet. She shivered again and lifted her arms, looping them loosely around him in offering. When she felt his muscles bunching beneath her palms, she stroked them, following hard curves and hollows down toward the small of his back, where she marveled over a new discovery. In the dip there, she felt a soft, thin tuft of fur, so masculine, so perfect.

He trembled a bit as she stroked him there, then dipped one finger beneath the waistband of his jeans.

He mumbled something against the upper curve of her breast, and then with a quick movement, he released the clasp of her bra, allowing her to tumble free.

The throbbing at her center reached new heights as lightning seemed to zing along her nerves, every new sensation headed toward her core as if it was all that existed.

The air grew thin in the room, and she panted helplessly, her head falling back, her eyes closing, giving herself to the moment and to him as she had seldom given herself before: mindlessly, helplessly. If any part of her didn't ache in that throbbing, primal rhythm, she had long since ceased to be aware of it.

Here and now. Everything else vanished.

* * *

Wade felt the moment when she left the world behind, her entire consciousness focused on what was happening inside her. He wasn't far behind, but he struggled against his own hardening body, the pounding demands of his own needs.

Because he wanted to be sure to give it all to her, everything. He couldn't explain it, maybe didn't want to look too closely. All he knew was that he wanted to brand himself on this woman, right here and now in a way she would never forget.

So when she reached for the clasp of his jeans, moaning softly, he stopped her. Instead he reached for her shorts and panties, and tugged them down with one hand just as his mouth found her pebbled nipple and drew it deeply inside. He sucked gently at first, but as she pressed herself harder against him, he threw gentleness to the wind and sucked on her as if he could draw her right inside him.

The groan that escaped her fueled his own needs, and he had to push them back. If this woman remembered nothing else about him, she was going to remember this night, these hours.

Something even more primal than need for satisfaction drove him. This was a claiming of some kind, a claim he had never tried to make before. And for some reason, that need to claim added to his passion, making him almost as desperate as he was hungry.

The damn shorts and panties flew away at last, tugged off her ankles as he swept her up in one arm, his mouth still latched to her breast, each movement of his tongue and lips sending a fresh quiver through her.

She was clinging to him now, clinging as tightly as she could manage to his back, and the feel of her arms hanging on to him was surely the most wonderful thing he had ever felt. More wonderful even than the acts to come.

He'd have gone to the stake before he would ever admit how long it had been since someone's arms had been around him, or how good it felt, or how much he needed it.

He almost didn't want to lower her to the bed.

But his body had already made promises to her, and he was going to keep every one of them.

He laid her down, cast aside the rest of his clothing, pausing only to tug some protection from his pocket. He hadn't anticipated this, hadn't anticipated any sexual relationship at all, but the military had taught him well. He always carried protection, and for the first time he was truly grateful for it because it would ensure no harm came to Cory from him.

He tossed the packets on the bedside table. Then he wrapped his arms around the naked beauty beside him, and felt her arms wrap around him, and had the craziest feeling that he could stay right here, right now forever.

Their bodies met, warm smooth skin against warm smooth skin, their legs tangled, working for even greater closeness.

But he had promises to keep. With mouth and hands he began to explore her, every inch of her, stealing all her secrets even as he lifted her to moaning heights of passion. Then his mouth followed his hands, across her belly, her hips, down the insides of her thighs to the delicate arches of her feet.

He could think of no better way to worship her than by kissing her every inch.

The pounding in his loins now hammered in his brain. Slowly he slipped up over her, smelling her wonderful musky scent, then dipping his mouth and tongue into her most private places.

Claiming. Branding. Possessing.

Causing her to arch upward with a soft scream as he touched the delicate knot of nerves that gave so much pleasure-pain. She tasted good. So good. This was something he had almost never shared, it seemed so intimate to him, and he knew just the barest moment of fear he might not be doing it right, but her body immediately answered as if it had heard his question.

Oh, it was so right. So good. He licked, nibbled, tasted, even plunged his tongue deep into her, and felt a smile stretch his lips when her hands grabbed his head, pressing him closer still, then clawed at his shoulders as if she could barely stand the pleasure.

He felt the ripping shudder as an orgasm took her, listened to her moan helplessly, then before the riptide had fully passed, he pulled on a condom and moved up over her, staking his claim completely as he slid into her warm, welcoming depths.

"Wade!" Half sigh, half cry, and never had his name sounded so beautiful. Triumph filled him in that moment, because she was his, all his.

Then the throbbing in his body demanded more, her hands tugged at him, trying to move him, and when at last he began to thrust, she sighed his name again, wrapped her arms around his back and her legs around his hips.

Holding him. Hugging him with her entire being. Making him welcome in every way as she carried him with her to the stars.

For that little while, he even allowed himself to believe he could belong.

# Chapter 11

They lay together for a long time, just cuddling. That was something new to him, too. And he liked it. Finally he decided to tell her so, even though he was aware it could make her dislike him, to know how casually he had treated sex in his past. But for some odd reason, he was telling Cory lots of things he'd never told anyone else. Maybe because she always seemed to understand.

"This is the first time," he said slowly.

He felt a ripple pass through her and when he peered at her face in the nearly total dark, he thought he saw a smile. "What's so funny?"

"Turn on a light," she suggested. "I want to see your face, too."

Exposure. Confidences were easier in the dark, as he'd learned sitting in an awful lot of hides in alien lands. But he obliged her, turning on the small lamp beside the bed. It was dim, just enough light to read by.

She was smiling at him with puffy lips and puffy eyes, and he had to admit she looked happier than he'd yet seen her. "Nothing's funny," she said in answer to his question. "I just don't think this is the first time you've made love to a woman."

"Oh. That isn't what I meant." And now he half wished he hadn't mentioned it at all.

"Then what?" Her smile slipped away, her gaze grew gentle.

He hesitated. "First time I ever cuddled after."

Her eyes widened, and for an instant she looked as if she didn't understand. But when she did, something happened on her face that seemed to reach out and touch his heart.

"Oh, Wade," she said softly, and all of a sudden her arms wound around him, hanging on tightly, so tightly, and giving him that feeling again. "Oh, Wade, I think that's the saddest thing I've ever heard."

"No...no, don't be sad. Be happy. I am."

She burrowed her face into his shoulder, and he felt her kiss him there. "You," she whispered, "are more special than you know."

"So are you."

She didn't answer, just tightened her hold on him even more.

He would have liked to stay there forever, and maybe if he'd been an ordinary guy, he could have done so. But he was a former SEAL, and coded into him now was a mission clock, one that wouldn't stop ticking. He couldn't forget reality for long, couldn't forget there might be a killer out there circling in even now. Couldn't forget that even alarm systems were little protection against a determined assassin. He ought to know: he'd disabled more than one.

So finally, feeling as if he were ripping off his own skin, he gave in to the demands of reality. "Let's take a shower," he said. A gentle way to ease them back. To stay as they were left them with few defenses. He might not be at a total disadvantage naked, but he couldn't say the same for Cory. And if they got distracted again—a very tempting possibility—they could miss something important.

So they showered together, playing games with a bar of soap and a nylon puff that neither had been designed for, but that made them both grin, and elicited some pleasurable sighs.

He helped towel her dry, then slipped from the bathroom while she worked a bit at her hair. His internal clock and other triggers were beginning to drive him nuts. He'd allowed himself to be off duty for too long.

A quick check of the alarm showed him nothing amiss, but he crept through the house anyway, once again putting his knife on his belt, donning boots because protecting the feet was so essential. He skipped the shirt, though, as the house was warm enough. Cory would just have to live with the sight of the knife.

When he was sure the house was still secure, he followed the glow of light to the kitchen and found Cory making coffee. He glanced at the clock. "A little late for coffee. Or maybe awfully early, depending."

She shook her head, and when she faced him, he could tell that reality had settled in once again for her, too. All the softness was gone, except, perhaps, for her eyes when they brushed over him.

Until they came to rest on the knife.

"I see," was all she said, and turned her back again, waiting for the coffee. "I didn't think we'd get much sleep. One way or the other."

"No," he admitted. "Cory, I'm sorry."

"Stop apologizing, damn it. It's not your fault all this is happening. It's not your fault I'm such a mess. So we took a vacation. At least I did. For a little while I felt normal, I'm not going to apologize for it, and okay, now we face the real world again."

"You *are* normal."

"Oh, let's not get back on that again. Look at what I did today. I freaked out, basically. I totally shut down. Then I took it out on you."

Turning, she grabbed two mugs and put them on the table. Then she got out the milk. A burst of steam announced the coffeemaker was pretty much done.

He watched, feeling an unaccustomed pain in his chest. A few minutes later, when they sat at the table, he spoke again. "Quit feeling bad about what you said to me."

"Why shouldn't I feel bad? I was horrid. I'm surprised you could even want to make love to me after that."

This was not good. He didn't want her to feel this way about herself. Not at all. Not ever. How could he make it clear to her that he really had forgotten what she had said?

Finally he chose his words with care. "I've had a lot of time to develop confidence in myself and who I am. The names don't stick anymore. I've been called far worse. I'm not saying I'm perfect. God knows, that's the last thing I'd say about myself. But I have had time to build and internalize a lot of confidence over the last twenty years. You haven't. You got stripped of everything, and now you've got a bunch of broken pieces to work with. Of course you're going to strike out sometimes. But you'll do just fine. You'll find a new version of yourself. If anything, I hope you do it better than I did."

"Meaning?"

"Maybe you can get rid of some of the trip wires."

At that she laughed unsteadily. "I don't even know where any of mine are."

"Sure you do. You know what makes you uneasy, you know what scares you. You even told me what made you feel threatened."

"I did?"

"Hope," he said simply. "You're terrified to hope."

Long minutes passed in silence as Cory faced what he was saying. It was as if his simple statement had stripped away everything else and forced her to look at what might be the deepest wound of all. And it hurt. She finally covered her lower face with her hand and closed her eyes. "I used to take hope for granted."

"I know. You will again."

He sounded so sure, but considering how long she'd been living without it, and how much its reemergence scared her, she wasn't sure about that. What did she have to hope for, after all? That one morning she'd wake up and discover that her life was free of threat, that she could then take up the strands of the woman she had once been?

She'd never be that woman again. Ever. And in the murkiness of now, she couldn't even imagine who she might become if the threat was removed.

"First," he said, "it's little things. Immediate things. Little hopes. Just seeds."

"Do you hope?"

"Hell yeah. I hope for lots of things, some big, some small."

"Such as?"

"I hope I can settle into civilian life at least enough that I'm not a ticking time bomb just waiting to be startled. I hope someday I get past this edginess and stop seeing every shadow as a place of concealment. I hope that I can sleep without waking in a cold sweat from nightmares."

"You do that, too?"

"All the time. Not as much as even a few months ago, but yeah."

"Me, too. For a long time I was afraid to sleep."

"I can imagine."

"For a long time I nearly jumped out of my skin at the sound of a knock."

"But it's better now?"

"Yes. It is."

"You see?" He spread his hands. "Baby steps, Cory. You've already started to take them. It's been my experience, though, that you'll take a few backward steps along the way."

"I think I took a big one today."

"No."

"No? What do you call what I did? That…that thousand-yard stare you called it. That numbness. That recklessness. Then yelling at you."

"The yelling was you coming back. I've seen guys go a lot deeper and stay there a lot longer. You actually had a pretty fast turnaround."

"And that's good?"

"You bet. There's a lot of life left in you, Cory. You're starting to kick the traces of fear and despair. It'll be rough for a while, but I believe you'll do it."

"I hope so." Then a little laugh slipped out of her. "I hope so. Listen to me."

"Sounds good." He stirred in the chair, and he seemed to lean forward, toward her. "You may have gone through more healing in the last year than you really realize. I don't know. I'm no shrink. I can only tell you what I've seen, and what I've learned from my own experience."

"I'm tired of being such a mess all the time."

"Tell me about it. But look at you. You're still here.

You're still trying to deal. You could have quit a long time ago."

"I don't know."

"No way I can judge. But ask yourself, have you been living in terror every single minute of the last year you've been here?"

She started to say yes, then realized that wasn't entirely true. Her heart skipped a beat with the understanding, for it surprised her. Maybe what she thought of herself wasn't exactly true. "At first, yes. But then only when something happened to worry me. I can't say I spent the whole year in shaking terror."

"No, I'd bet most of the time you let it slide to the back of your mind. When nothing threatened you directly, when you were working."

She nodded slowly. "That's true."

"So the idea that you spent a year doing nothing but living in terror is your perception. Basically it was the story you told yourself, but maybe not exactly what you were doing."

"No, it's true," she said, straightening a little. "I'd forget about it. Maybe not for too long at one time, but I did. I *had* to."

"Of course you did. So give yourself a little credit here, Cory. In some pretty awful circumstances, having lost everything that meant anything to you, you managed to function. To hold a job, pay the bills, read books, maybe go to a movie. You kept going. You were probably doing a whole lot better than you thought."

"No. No, I wasn't." She still remembered all too vividly her many failures. And there were scores of them. Things undone, things unsaid. If she sat down and made a list, she'd hate herself.

"So sure? You didn't quit. A lot of people would have.

Granted, healing probably would have been easier, maybe even happened faster, if you hadn't been cut off from everything. But that only makes what you've achieved all the more admirable."

"I haven't achieved anything!"

"Getting through the past year on your own is a huge achievement. Why don't you count your strengths instead of your weaknesses for a change?"

That comment drew her up short. Her strengths? She'd been looking at herself for a year as a quivering blob of fear, incapable of answering her own door without peeking out first to see who was there.

"You went to work, didn't you? You went to the bank, and the grocery store. You even made a few friends."

"Not really. I couldn't let anyone get too close."

"But was that a failing or a reasonable caution given what you went through?"

She almost wanted to protest that he didn't know her well enough to guess what she had been like for the past year. And yet, she found herself drawn up short by awareness, a shift of perspective on her own actions and behavior. Yes, she had lived with fear, but not enough fear that it had prevented her from functioning. Not enough that it had kept her locked in this house.

Going to work hadn't caused her a nervous breakdown, although she'd never dropped her guard about what she said. Yes, answering her door had been difficult, but considering what had come through her door that night fifteen months ago, maybe it was surprising she could answer a door at all. She'd had dinner a few times with Nate and Marge Tate, with Gage and Emma Dalton. She went to the library regularly, and never considered avoiding it, at least not since the first few weeks.

Maybe she was confusing heightened caution with

terror, at least later. There was no question she had been terrified right after Jim was killed. No question she had been terrified when she had finally been dropped here on her own. But of course she had been. For the first time in months she didn't have a Marshal at her elbow, had to venture out on her own, pick up the threads of the basic necessities of life.

And she had done it. Unhappily, with her heart so broken it sometimes seemed too painful to draw a breath, hating it and fearing the unknown that loomed before her as much as the past that might try to follow her. But she had done it.

"You see?" he said, almost as if he sensed the shift in her. "What happened today has probably happened to you a number of times since your husband was killed. You disconnected because it was too much. The past, the present, all of it converged on you again when you listened to Gage and me talking. So you shut down. That's an important protective thing. Sometimes it's the only way we can deal."

"You do it, too?"

"I thought I said so. And God knows I've seen enough people do it. You see it in survivors all the time. Survivors of battle, survivors of natural disasters. That's the thing. It's like the brain gets so overloaded it just says *enough*. It can't deal, so it basically removes you as far as it can. It's not a failing. It's not something wrong with a person. It's *survival*. It's only a bad thing when it takes over for too long and too completely."

"But you said post-traumatic stress disorder. Isn't that an illness?"

"But that's not what I saw today, Cory. PTSD, yes, but the useful, coping kind. I guess what I'm trying to get at is that after watching you, especially today, I don't think you're as bad off as you think."

She sighed, letting his words sink in slowly, rearranging her mental and emotional furniture, trying to see herself in a more positive light. The change left her feeling uneasy. Then a new thought occurred to her, one that caused her a pang.

"Maybe you're right about survivor guilt."

He stirred again. "What do you mean?"

"It hasn't been just fear and grief. Maybe I've been punishing myself with both of them." Even as she could accept the emotional logic of that, she didn't like the idea much. She almost hoped he would deny it.

"Could be, I suppose. But now you're getting into shrink territory, and I've probably already ventured too far that way. I'm just talking from what I've seen and experienced over the years."

She turned the idea around in her head, though, weighing it against her emotional response. The Marshals had tried to give her everything she needed to move forward in a safe life. If she looked at the past year honestly, they had succeeded. But she had refused to fully accept the gift. Grieving had been one thing. Even some initial fear at being on her own. But at some point had she started using fear as a way to flagellate herself and limit her options because she was still alive when Jim and her baby were not?

It was as if doors were finally opening in her mind, giving her a different view than the box she had tried to paint around herself during the past year.

Plenty of food for thought, and plenty to leave her feeling adrift inside herself. Who was she, actually? And what had she really been doing with herself over the past year? She suspected these new ideas of herself might be closer to the mark than the abbreviated form she had adopted previously. Grief and fear did not begin to explain it all.

She sighed. "I've got a lot of thinking to do. But I'd appreciate it if you would accept my apology for what I said earlier. I'm horrified at myself."

"I thought I already had. Apology accepted."

"You're a very kind man."

He said nothing for a while, and she wondered if she had offended him somehow. Then he said, an almost rueful note of humor in his voice, "I think I need to learn how to accept a compliment."

"Does it bother you that I said you're kind?" How awful if it did, because he had certainly been kind to her, kinder than she had any right to expect.

He answered, still sounding rueful. "My mind is trying to remind me of all the times I wasn't kind."

At that a forlorn little laugh escaped her. "Yeah, the way I'm sitting here remembering all the ways I wasted the last year. All the things I could have done but didn't."

"I'll cut myself some slack if you will."

"Deal." But was it? Could she really see herself through his eyes, rather than her own? He certainly made a compelling case for a Cory who had acted the way most people would after what she had been through, rather than the Cory she had talked herself into thinking she was.

Then she asked a question that she knew was freighted with baggage. But it was a question that needed an answer because it might help her plant one of those seeds of hope he had talked about, give her something to hang on to.

"Wade?"

"Yes?"

"Tell me just one little hope you have right now. Just one little thing, not the big things."

She watched as his face started to freeze, but before

he could turn completely to stone again, she watched him relax his expression muscle by muscle. For a full minute, he didn't say anything.

"Wade?"

"I hope that you'll hug me again sometime," he said finally.

He couldn't have sent a surer shaft straight into her heart. Aching for him, for his isolation and loneliness, she rose and rounded the table. He pushed back as if to rise, but before he could she slid onto his lap and wrapped her arms around him tightly.

"I hope," she whispered tremulously, "that you'll let me hug you again lots of times. It feels so good to me."

He wrapped his arms snugly around her in answer. "Anytime, Cory. Anytime."

The skin-crawling sensation came back, possibly because he'd gone AWOL for a few hours. Or it returned because he sensed something internally. Some inner clock was ticking, counting out the minutes and hours it would take for the killer to respond if he had identified Cory.

The sensation had never failed him when there was danger, had rarely been wrong about danger that didn't exist.

The sun would rise in less than an hour. This was the time of attack, when darkness still provided a cloak and most humans were at their weakest. This was the hour when many a guard lost his alertness, when sleep stole awareness no matter how hard one tried to stay awake.

The hour before dawn.

Maybe that's all it was. But he counted back through his mind, first the phone call, then the stranger who drove two different cars. Maybe he was to be the killer himself. Or he was merely the assassin's lookout, an unidentifiable face that should have passed unnoticed while collecting information.

Damn, he wished he knew.

He had at last persuaded Cory to doze on the couch, promising he would be right there and awake. But he wished he could slip out and sweep the perimeter, because no matter how well the sheriff's deputies did the job, he could do it better himself.

He checked the alarm more than once, making sure it hadn't been disconnected. No warnings showed on the status display.

The phone rang. He grabbed it immediately, hoping the single ring wouldn't disturb Cory. She sighed but remained asleep, exhausted and trusting him.

God, he hoped he was worthy of that trust.

He slipped into the kitchen with it, after the barest of greetings, and heard Gage's voice. Through the kitchen curtains, he could see the pale light of dawn.

"We identified the guy you saw with the two different cars," Gage said. He sounded barely awake himself.

"Yeah? Who?"

"A private detective out of Denver."

"Hell."

"Exactly. I've got the Denver P.D. going to roust him and find out who he was working for."

"Like I can't imagine."

"This could be good. At least we'll know exactly what info he passed on, and who he passed it to."

"Yeah. Maybe we can even use him." Wade's brain slipped into high gear and he refilled his coffee mug. The more he thought about it, the better he liked this setup.

"That was my thought," Gage said. "If it's not too late. But first I have to question him. He'll be cooperative if he wants to keep his license."

"How long is that going to take?"

"I'm going to start with a phone interview once Denver picks him up. I'll let you know. Don't let her out of the house for now."

"I won't. Listen, Gage?"

"Yeah?"

"I gotta get some sleep, man. Four hours."

"I'll send Sara Ironheart over in mufti. Like for coffee. Give me an hour. I can also put eyes on the house, but that might take a little longer so we don't give the game away."

"Absolutely don't give the game away. We've got to end this."

"I agree. Can you make it another hour?"

"I'm fine. But I'll be better on a little sleep."

He hung up and rubbed his eyes. A private dick, huh? Someone who wouldn't know the story, could be fed a line of bull. Someone unrelated to the case who could be sent here to find Cory without setting off alarms. In theory, anyway.

This killer was no tyro at this. No tyro at all. The palms of his hands started itching as he thought of all the things he'd like to do to the assassin. Things he knew he'd never do because he was an ordinary citizen now.

But there were hundreds of ways a man could die, and in his experience few of them were quick or merciful.

With a shake of his head, he pushed the thoughts away. He wasn't that man anymore. In fact, he was trying to become a very different man. One who might actually be worthy of breathing the same air as a woman like Cory Farland.

One thing he did know for certain. He would do whatever it took to keep Cory safe. Even if it meant spending the rest of his life in hell.

# Chapter 12

Sara Ironheart arrived with the gentlest of taps on the window beside the front door. She wore a heavy jacket, overshirt and jeans, and from its concealment flashed her badge. He also caught a glimpse of a 9mm semiautomatic in a shoulder holster.

Cringing because it would undoubtedly wake Cory, Wade turned off the alarm and let her in. Then he turned the alarm on as quickly as possible, hating that damn beep.

"Wade?" Cory called drowsily.

"I'm here," he called back. "Everything's fine. Get some more sleep."

She mumbled something, and from the doorway he watched her turn a bit on the couch and slip back into slumber. This woman, he thought, wasn't anywhere near the scared kitten she thought herself.

He motioned Sara to follow him into the kitchen,

and closed the door on the hallway so their conversation wouldn't disturb Cory more.

"Thanks for coming."

"Least I can do." A beautiful woman with raven-black hair that was highlighted by just a few threads of silver, she gave him a half smile. "Gage filled me in. You go to sleep."

"Coffee's over there, mugs in the cupboard above."

"Thanks."

"Four hours max," he cautioned her.

She nodded. "I'll wake you."

Then, sentry in place, he went back to the living room and made himself as comfortable as he could on the recliner.

An adrenaline jolt tried to keep him from sleeping, but this was a battle he'd fought and won many times. A man couldn't survive his job without learning to sleep anytime, anywhere, even standing bolt upright. And the recliner was a hell of an improvement over that.

A couple of minutes later he'd quieted his body, and sleep slipped over him. A light sleep.

For even as he dozed, his ears never quit working, cataloguing every sound as either normal or not.

It was another one of those survival things.


Cory awoke, a warm, lovely dream giving way to instant panic. Someone was in the house.

"Shh," a voice said quietly, and she opened her eyes to see Sara Ironheart squatting beside her. "It's okay. I'm spelling Wade."

Cory drew a shuddering breath, managing a nod as her racing heart started to settle from a terrified gallop to something closer to normal.

"Coffee?" Sara whispered.

Cory nodded and pushed herself upright. When she saw Wade dozing in the recliner, everything inside her turned warm and soft. The gifts he had given her during the night hours seemed to have settled in and taken root. She felt good, despite the reminder of the threat that Sara represented.

She rose as quietly as she could and followed Sara to the kitchen.

"He sleeps lightly," Sara remarked. "Reminds me of my cat. His ears almost twitch at every sound, even when his eyes don't open."

Cory smiled. "He's amazing."

"I could tell you were starting to wake, getting restless. I didn't mean to scare you, but I didn't want you to realize someone else was here without knowing immediately who I was."

"Thanks. I appreciate that." She filled her own mug and topped Sara's. They sat together at the kitchen table. "So what's going on?"

"Wade said he needed to catch some sleep, so Gage sent me over. That's all."

"Yeah, he was up all night." She didn't explain her part in that, but she supposed Sara could put the pieces together.

Then another thought struck her. "If he didn't feel comfortable sleeping without someone here on guard, something must have happened."

"I honestly don't know." Sara smiled ruefully. "My brother-in-law—you've met Micah?"

"I've seen him around."

"Well, he used to be special forces, and I've seen him get antsy at times, as if he senses something but doesn't quite know what. Even after all these years he'll still go into a hypervigilant mode at times. Don't ask me to explain what gets them going. It's like they have some kind of internal radar for when something is off-kilter. Or gathering."

"Is he often right?"

"Let's just say I've been glad more than once to have him on my team, as well as a member of the family."

Cory nodded slowly. "It must be hard on them, though."

"I can't say. It's been my experience they don't talk a whole lot about it." Sara's smile was almost wry. "Sometimes I think they get hooked into some kind of mystical cosmic-information highway. Like when my son broke his arm. Micah started getting worked up the day before Sage fell out of the tree. Said he could feel something was going to happen."

"Wow." Cory tried to imagine it.

"Other times, on the job mostly, he's tried to explain it as some kind of internal countdown clock. If $X$ happened, then $Y$ should happen within a certain time frame." Sara shrugged. "I don't know. I'm just a cop, but I guess I have my own form of the same thing. Hunches. Little niggles. The feeling that something isn't right."

"Good intuition."

"Whatever you call it." Sara glanced at the clock. "Wade made me promise four hours and not a second longer. So I'll wake him a little after ten."

"He could sleep longer," Cory protested. They were still keeping their voices low, so it was hard to put enough emphasis into the words. "He needs it."

"When a man like that says four hours, he means it. I'm not going there."

Nor, Cory decided, would she. Wade could be determined about some things, and she had already nearly made him walk out with some nasty words. Who knew how he'd respond to direct defiance, even a little one like this.

Only he probably wouldn't see it as little. He had undertaken to protect her, and she supposed he would have good reason to get hopping mad if she broke his rules.

And she'd be foolish not to cooperate with her protector, even over something so small.

A sigh escaped her, and she began to feel a bit as she had when the Marshals had kept her in the safe house those three months. Trapped, watched, with no volition. At least this time she had moved past mourning. Mostly.

But events roused the old memories, and she sat there with her hands wrapped around her coffee mug, forcing herself to sort through them.

The loss of Jim and the baby still ached, but more like a tooth that had been treated than one that had a raging infection. It would probably always hurt. But as Wade had showed her, she could live again, if she committed to it. Committed to moving on and taking whatever little joys came her way, instead of feeling guilty about them.

Once she got this killer off her back.

Even that, she realized, was a choice she was making. Would she let that man's desire to protect himself keep her always one step removed from truly living? Or would she take charge of her own life again?

Because nobody, nobody, had a promise that they would see tomorrow. She surely ought to have learned that the hard way. She was here now only because a gunshot had failed to kill her, too.

Borrowed time? Maybe. Or maybe this was just life and it was time to stand up and participate again.

A half hour later, Cory went in to wake Wade. It was the first time she had seen him wake, and she was fascinated. At first his eyes snapped open and he tensed, as if ready to spring, but the instant he saw her, his face softened. "Everything okay?" he asked.

"Everything's fine. Sara's getting ready to go."

"Okay." He passed his hand over his face and sat up. Then he wrapped his arms around her hips and pressed his face to her belly. Instantly warm tingles awoke in her center. Reaching out, she ran her hand over his short hair.

"One of these days," he muttered.

"One of these days what?"

He sighed, then tipped his head back and smiled at her. "One of these days we're going to have all the time we want alone together."

She smiled, liking the sound of that. "I'll hold you to it."

"Good."

But then he let go of her, and the guardian returned, flattening his face, steeling his eyes. He pushed out of the chair and went with her to the kitchen, where Sara was donning her jacket to conceal her gun. She looked like just anyone, nothing giving away that she was a deputy.

"Okay, then," she said with a smile. "I'll be off."

At that moment there was a knock at the door. They all stiffened. Cory's heart slammed. That sound would probably always make her heart slam.

"Let me get it," Wade said.

But Sara was right on his heels, gun magically appearing. She stood back, holding the pistol in a two-handed grip, waiting, while Wade looked out the window beside the door. Cory peered around the edge of the kitchen door, gripping the frame so tightly her knuckles turned white.

"Gage," Wade said.

He opened the door to the sheriff, and Cory almost gasped in amazement. Gage didn't look anything like himself. No, he looked like a man who could have lived on the streets undercover for DEA, as he once had: utterly disreputable in a worn leather jacket, stained jeans and a ball cap rather than his usual Stetson.

"Hi," he said as he stepped inside. "Sorry, but I didn't want it to look like the sheriff was stopping in."

"You sure don't," Cory managed.

Gage chuckled. "Good. Okay, we've got plenty to talk about now."

Sara spoke. "Want me to stay?"

"Oh, yeah. We've got some planning to do."

The living room was the only place where they could all sit. Gage took the recliner, Sara the rocker, leaving the couch for Cory and Wade.

Cory's heart had begun to beat a little nervously, knowing Gage wouldn't be here unless he had learned something.

"Okay," he said. "I told Wade earlier, and I don't know if he had a chance to tell you, Cory, but the guy he saw that he thought might be tailing you was a private detective from Denver." Reaching into one of his pockets, he pulled out a notebook and flipped it open. "I'll try to stick to just what you need to know."

"Okay." Her heart skipped then beat a bit faster. Her mouth started to dry with anticipated fear.

"His client, who is going by the name of Vincent Ordano, hired him to find you under the pretext that you had embezzled a huge sum of money from him. He claimed he could track you only as far as this county, that you seemed to have changed your appearance and name, and the only way to flush you out was to make you think you'd been found. Just as Wade suggested might be the strategy."

Cory felt her stomach turn over, and she covered her mouth with her hand, as if that could somehow help.

"Anyway, as Wade suspected, again, the investigator, Moran, scoped out women of a certain age group who had moved here within the last year. He found eight of you, and since Ordano couldn't be sure which of you it was, Moran made the phone call and watched the reactions. He settled on you and your friend Marsha, for exactly the reasons Wade suspected. Moran saw that Marsha got a dog, but he was far more concerned about Wade appearing out of nowhere in your life. That struck him as a whole lot odder than buying a dog. My apologies."

"There's nothing to apologize for," Cory said.

"No? Maybe not. None of us thought you taking a roomer would be pulling some kind of trigger. Regardless, Moran then started some background checking. Marsha, of course, had a trail he could follow all the way back. Yours was sketchy enough to make him think you might be the one hiding."

A soft sound of distress escaped Cory. Wade immediately took her hand, but at the moment it proved to be scant comfort. "It was that easy?"

"Only because someone, somewhere, pointed Ordano to this county," Gage reminded her. "And that's something we are definitely going to deal with as soon as we get Ordano."

"How are we going to do that?"

"That's what we're going to discuss. But let me finish up here, because there's actually some good news in this morass."

Cory managed a nod, and tightened her grip on Wade's hand.

"Moran hasn't reported back yet to Ordano that he's sure you're the woman Ordano wants. He only finished his background checks late last night, and we caught him this morning before he even got to his office. To say the guy is appalled would be an understatement, so we have his full cooperation."

"But if he knows where Ordano is…"

"He doesn't. Their communications have all been by phone and email, and services were paid for with a credit card by phone. We assume Ordano must be nearby, but we don't know exactly where. I'm tracing activity on the credit card Moran was given, but the information may well be out-of-date by the time we get it. If there is any. He might not even be using that card anymore, or any other cards under that name. Hell, we don't know that he really *is* Vincent Ordano. I've got folks researching him, but they may well come up empty-handed."

Cory tried to swallow but her mouth was too dry.

"And I am not, I repeat *not*, going to call the Marshals on this." Gage's frown was deep and dark. "I don't know who talked, but someone evidently did, and until I find out, this stays here, in this county, among my people."

"I agree," Wade said flatly. "The least little slip could start the clock ticking again. I don't want Cory having to live any longer in fear."

"Absolute agreement here," Gage said. "We take care of our own in this county, and Cory has been through more than enough."

Cory actually felt her throat tighten. She was part of this county now, this place she had tried not to connect with. An unexpected homecoming in the midst of this mess. Yes, she wanted to stay here, and she would do whatever was necessary.

"For the moment," Gage continued, "we have an advantage. Moran hasn't identified Cory to Ordano.

That means we can arrange an ambush and substitute a stand-in."

"No." The word came out Cory's mouth almost before she was aware of it.

Everyone looked at her.

"No one is going to risk their life for me. Absolutely not."

"Cory," Wade started to say.

"No." The determination that filled her now was unshakable. "Don't you see? I have enough to live with. I couldn't live with it if someone was hurt or killed in my place. What's more, I think I need to do this. I need to face this guy. I'll never be free of fear again unless I do this." She wondered if she could even convey how strongly she felt that this was something she had to do to lay to rest some of her demons for good. How could you explain that you had run long enough, and now it was time to stand your ground?

But instead of endless argument, she was surprised because all three of them seemed to understand what she was trying to say.

"Okay," Gage said, and Wade nodded, albeit with obvious reluctance. "We'll set up an ambush. Since I want Cory in armor, we need to set it up to occur at night when she can reasonably wear a jacket to conceal the armor. I'm thinking the supermarket parking lot. It would be reasonable for Cory to leave work a half hour or so after the store is closed, and to leave apparently alone. Yet there are plenty of places around where we can conceal ourselves. There are always cars out there overnight for example. A Dumpster. Some trees. Rooftops. The trick will be making sure we don't pick a hiding place that Ordano would choose."

Wade spoke. "Give me a thousand-yard sight line, and I won't miss."

Gage's head tilted a bit. "Are you asking me to deputize you?"

"If it'll make this work better. At least make sure I'm on a roof somewhere with an unhindered sight line. In case."

Cory shuddered helplessly at what he was proposing. She didn't want him to have that on his conscience because of her. She didn't think she could stand it.

Sara spoke. "Micah's a trained sniper, too."

"So put both of us out there. It'll reduce the number of people you need on the ground, and thus reduce the number of people who might give us away."

Gage nodded slowly. "Okay. I like it. I'll go set it up, and give Moran his story to pass along. I'll see if I can't get him to do it in a way that'll push Ordano to move quickly. We can't afford to give him a lot of time to plan."

Cory spoke through stiff lips. "If what happened that night he came after my husband is any indication, he's not one for a lot of planning. He may be good at covering his tracks, but there were so many other times he could have gotten Jim when he was alone…" Her voice broke. "He didn't have to come into the condo when we were both there."

"Good point," Wade said, squeezing her hand gently. "The guy's an opportunist, and a bit careless. He chose an easy way to get at your husband at a time when escape would also be easy, with no one out and about to notice him. And he didn't care about collateral damage, obviously."

He paused a moment, then added, "This Ordano may think of himself as an assassin, but I'd give him low marks. My bet is he's an ordinary thug who took the job for money, and that he doesn't have a whole lot of experience."

Cory looked at him. "How could you know that?"

"Because I would have done it cleaner, and you wouldn't have been around."

The words chilled Cory, but she looked into those dark eyes of his, and she saw a whisper of the pain he felt because he had been required to do such things in his past. She ached for him, for the burdens he carried in silence, for the duty that had scarred him. It raised him even higher in her estimation that he couldn't shrug off such things, that she could see the ghosts in his gaze.

"All right," she said, as if everything had been settled. "Just tell me where to be, and when, and exactly what you want me to do. But let me make it perfectly clear, I will not let anyone take the risk in my place. I cannot live with that. I will not live with that."

Gage sighed and nodded. "I get it, Cory. And sometimes we have to face our demons head-on. It's the only way to be free."

That was it in a nutshell. It didn't mean that she'd sleep any better until this was over. It didn't mean her heart would stop galloping.

But she had to stand up for herself. Now. This time. No matter the cost.

Gage and Sara left like a couple, arms linked, heads bowed together and talking as they walked down the street a little way to Sara's battered pickup. Keeping up the pretense, just in case.

*Just in case.*

The words seemed to hang in her mind like smoke long after a fire has burned out. They had to assume that Moran was Ordano's only information source, but they had to assume at the same time that he was not. No chances, no unnecessary risks.

And Cory felt as if the house were closing in on her, just as those safe houses had a year ago. Only now that she had lost it completely did she realize just how much freedom she had exercised in the past year despite her fear. Freedom to run to the store. Freedom to sit in her backyard on a warm evening. Simple things, but huge in their absence.

"We'll take care of this soon," Wade told her. They were both pacing like caged animals, which might have amused her at another time. Right now it wasn't even remotely funny.

"What if he gets away?"

"He won't."

She faced him. "You can't promise that."

He stilled, becoming as motionless as a statue. "If he gets away, I promise you I will hunt him to the ends of the earth. He will not escape me."

Her chest tightened and began to ache. She reached out and seized his hand, clutching it between both of hers. "No, Wade. Promise me you won't do that. I couldn't stand it. I couldn't bear you to turn into that kind of hunter for me."

His gaze remained hard. "It wouldn't be the first time."

"Maybe not. But you've already done it for the last time. Promise me you won't do that for me. You've already served your time and done your duty. Now…now is for building, not destroying. Promise me, please."

His gaze never wavered. "I can't."

Then he turned from her and resumed his pacing.

Oh, God! She stood still, watching him, knowing there was not a thing she could say or do. This man would do his duty, however he perceived it, and that was that.

The only question was if she would accept it. Accept

him. As he was. As he had been. As he might have to become again.

And somewhere deep inside, she knew she already had.

# Chapter 13

Wade figured at most two days. His reasoning was straightforward. If Ordano was anywhere in the vicinity, he would move fast. Probably the very next night when Cory went to work. If he was halfway across the country, he might take another day.

"But no longer," he said. "This guy wants the threat removed, the faster the better."

Gage agreed.

Cory went to work at her usual time. Her shift seemed to drag. Gage had talked to her boss, so arrangements had been made so that Cory would leave the locked store alone at about a half hour past closing, while others remained inside, out of sight.

Even though she worried about the other employees, Cory was grateful that she would not have to spend that hour alone in an empty store, locked though it would be. Gage felt the presence of the other employees would prevent Ordano from trying to break in and take her out inside the store.

They were doing everything they could to ensure the attack happened in the parking lot. And all they wanted her to do was go in the back room, put on the body armor, pull her jacket over it, then leave the store. And if she saw Ordano, all they asked was that she drop to the ground and roll. Making herself small. Getting herself out of the way.

Walking bait. Exposing herself completely. Her skin crawled in anticipation, and as the hour grew closer, her heart accelerated and her stomach filled with nervous butterflies. She must have made a dozen trips to the fountain to ease the dryness in her mouth, but it only returned minutes later.

She knew the deputies were out there. She knew Wade was on some rooftop, deputized at least for a few days.

But worst of all was the way Wade had withdrawn again, turning into the stony man she had first met. No smile lightened his dark eyes. No unnecessary word passed his lips. He was gone from her as surely as if he had left town.

That hurt. It hurt so much that she now would have new baggage to deal with if she survived the next few days: the baggage of having fallen in love with a man who could shut her out as surely as if he had closed a door and locked it.

And she hurt for him, for the places this must be taking him back to, for all the memories it must be evoking. Right or wrong, duty or not, no soldier survived without scars. And every single one of his must have been ripped open by having to once again slip into the role he had chosen to protect her: Sniper. Killer. Hunter.

God, she almost wished Ordano had found her before

Wade ever appeared. She couldn't stand the thought of what he must be dealing with now.

The hour came at last. Her heart climbed into her throat as she looked at Betsy, her manager. The woman nodded, her face conveying fear and sorrow.

"Be careful."

Cory nodded. She went to the back room, climbed into the body armor and jacket then headed for the front door.

Betsy had given her a key so she could lock the door as she left. Gage didn't want to risk anyone else being visible through all that glass, because Ordano had proved he didn't care who he shot in addition to taking out his target.

The hair on the back of her neck was standing on end as Cory stepped out into a night that seemed strangely chilly for summer. Her entire back prickled with the sense of being watched as she turned and locked the front door from the outside.

But of course there were a dozen eyes on her right now, at the very least. Wade and Micah on the rooftops somewhere. Other deputies hiding in cars or elsewhere. Gage hadn't shared the details, nor did she especially want to know them.

Maybe those were deputies she spied sitting on the sidewalk in front of the pizza place four doors down, looking like two drunks sharing a bottle, totally ragged and sharing a torn blanket. How would she know?

They certainly sounded drunk, and argued over who had drunk the most of the bottle they passed between them.

Slowly she began to cross the parking lot. Per direction, she had left her car at the farthest end so she would have a longer walk. Giving Ordano more opportunity.

There were a half dozen other cars in the lot. Some probably occupied by deputies. All appearing empty.

She'd been ordered to avoid walking anywhere near any of them. Stay in the open. Stay away from those places of concealment.

Step after step she walked, her legs feeling like lead, her heart beating so loud she couldn't hear much else. Wandering a little to avoid the cars. Making loose shopping carts her excuse for the meandering walk, giving the attacker more opportunity to approach. Trying to make it necessary for him to leave his vehicle. If he was in one.

She glanced around again, but could see no heads in any of the cars. And of course, there was her own Suburban, a threat in itself, although she was sure it had been watched continuously since her arrival. She doubted anyone could have managed to hide himself in or around it.

At least, she had to believe that.

Another step. Grabbing another cart and shoving it toward a corral. Annoy the man, Gage had said. Make him impatient.

Well, there were certainly enough forgotten carts out here to help her do that.

She began to shiver, though she couldn't possibly be cold. Her legs went from lead to rubber, and she began to wonder if she would be able to make it all the way to her car.

Another cart. Turn around and walk it back. She clung to it for support even as she pushed it.

How had Wade lived like this for so long? She didn't think she could stand it for another ten minutes.

Maybe it wouldn't happen tonight. She was getting closer to her car, farther from the two guys sitting out in front of the pizza place. More isolated with every step.

"There you are."

She didn't recognize the voice. She froze, her fear ratcheting up to full-blown terror. Stiffly, she turned.

She recognized the face the instant she saw it. It was him. And he was pointing a gun at her from within the confines of a loose jacket. "You!" She gasped the word as she looked into a face that had haunted her nightmares.

"We're going to take a ride," he said. "A nice little ride, just the two of us."

That gun was pointed straight at her. Fear clouded her brain for a few seconds. Paralyzing her, making her forget what she was supposed to do.

"Move it," he said, his voice low and threatening.

But she couldn't move. Then, almost automatically, like any person faced with a gun, she started to obey.

No! The word shrieked in her brain. Drop and roll away. Drop and roll away.

For a few seconds she didn't think she'd be able to. It was as if her body had become a statue. But she might be blocking the sight line they had warned her about. And how would they know this was the guy if she didn't drop and roll? That was their signal that this was the one.

All of a sudden Wade's face popped into her mind. Somehow, thinking of him reminded her that she was capable. Not merely a frightened mouse, but a capable woman.

From his rooftop, Wade watched the encounter. He couldn't tell from the way Cory was acting if this was the guy, or just somebody who wanted to ask for directions. She stood there, still but yet standing, not doing the one thing they had told her to do.

Looking through the scope on the sniper rifle Gage had given him, he couldn't see enough. Cory blocked part of his view. And he couldn't shoot unless he was sure.

Damn!

He held his breath, hoping he didn't watch her get

murdered while he dithered about whether the target might not be the right guy. But he couldn't shoot until he was sure.

He glanced across the way to another rooftop where Micah lay, triangulating on the parking lot. The man seemed undecided, too.

Not enough info. He looked through his scope again, focusing, trying to see some defining detail. Only long experience kept him calm, his heartbeat steady. Forget it's Cory, he told himself. Don't let emotions get involved.

Stay calm. Steady breaths, finger on trigger, waiting. *Become ice.*

Then the two deputies in front of the pizza place started arguing loudly, in slurred voices. The man facing Cory turned just a bit. And Cory dropped to the ground.

It was him.

He held his breath and began to squeeze. But before he got off his shot, the loud pop of Micah's rifle pierced the night.

The guy dropped like a marionette whose strings had been cut. Wade waited, keeping a bead on him as the two "drunks" dropped bottle and blanket and charged across the lot toward Cory.

Only when they got there, and he could see through his scope that they kicked the guy's gun away and bent to cuff him, did Wade ease off on the trigger.

An explosive breath escaped him and he rolled over on his back, staring up at the star-studded heavens.

Thank God. Thank God.

Then the night erupted with colored lights and the sounds of sirens.

He could only lie there drained, thanking God. But a minute later, the adrenaline hit and he was up. He had to get to Cory. *Now.*

* * *

Cory was on her feet by the time Wade came charging up. Shaking from head to foot, she was staring down at the man who had killed her husband. It seemed he was still alive. She didn't know how she felt about that.

But then Wade's arms closed around her, and she was sure she had never felt anything more wonderful in her life. She sagged into his embrace and said his name over and over.

"Are you okay?" he demanded, clutching the back of her head and pressing her tightly to his chest.

She managed a nod.

Gage's voice reached her. "Take her home, Wade. We'll talk after I take care of this creep."

There wasn't an ounce of protest in her, and this time she didn't at all mind when Wade scooped her off her feet and carried her to her car. She hated it only when he let go of her after putting her in the passenger seat and buckling her in.

But when he climbed in beside her, and had turned over the ignition and shifted into gear, he reached over and grabbed her hand as if he were afraid it might slip away.

He carried her into the house, too. And this time when he turned off the alarm, he didn't turn it back on. No need now. From somewhere deep inside, a smile nearly rose to her lips. No more living in fear.

Wade stripped her of her jacket and the armor, then wrapped her chilled body in a blanket and settled her on the couch. "You need something hot to drink. Coffee? Something to eat?"

She doubted she could eat a thing. She still felt adrift, apart, as if she didn't quite belong in the here and now. "Coffee," she managed.

He went to start a pot, but came back immediately to sit

beside her, wrap her in his powerful arms and rub her to stimulate circulation. "Do you feel dizzy? Weak? Maybe you're in shock."

"I'm fine." Slowly, but surely, she realized she was. By the time the coffee was ready and he returned with two mugs, she actually smiled at him.

"I did it," she said.

And slowly, slowly, he smiled back, leaving the stony Wade behind, maybe for good. "You certainly did."

And for that moment, it was enough.

They cuddled throughout the night. First on the couch, then in her bed. Not making love, just cuddling and hugging. Little talking even, but as dawn began to lighten the world beyond the windows, Cory felt something she hadn't felt in a long time.

Pride. And exhilaration. She had done it. She had faced the killer. She had helped catch him.

It was her final act for Jim and their baby. The best memorial she could give them. But it was also the first act in her new life.

She bounded out of bed, and headed for the kitchen to make a huge breakfast, feeling hungry for food, but also hungry for life.

Wade followed, muttering something about a woman who didn't know when she had it good in a warm bed, but she laughed at his grumpiness until he laughed, too.

Oh, it was so good to hear him laugh. So good to feel like laughing.

She made mounds of scrambled eggs and hash browns, poured tall glasses of orange juice. And when they sat to eat, Wade said something that made her feel as light as a helium balloon.

"I'm so proud of you."

From him, that meant a whole lot. "I'm pretty proud of me, too."

"You should be."

She grinned at him and was thrilled when he grinned back.

"You make a mean hash brown, lady."

"Anytime." It felt good to cook for him, good to be doing something for someone else again. At the back of her mind lurked a little rain cloud, warning that there was no permanence here, that Wade would inevitably move on once he had settled whatever he had come here to settle with himself. But she didn't want to think about that now.

No, she was willing to toss her heart over the moon, and take the pain later, because it felt so good to be truly alive again, and life was nothing at all if you wouldn't take risks. A lesson she had learned all too well over the past year.

After they cleaned up, they took a walk together, and for the first time in forever, Cory noticed all the beauty around her, from the birdsong to the ceaseless breeze that whispered through the old tress lining the street. For the first time in a long time, she noticed that life was all around her.

Later they dozed for a while on the couch, for they'd been up most of the night, but then Gage dropped by, and the first of many questions got answered.

"Ordano is in the hospital under guard. The Marshals arrived this morning and the FBI will be here in a little while. The guy started talking as soon as he came out of anesthesia. If you care, Cory, we now know who hired him to kill your husband. And we know who gave you away."

"Who?"

"A secretary in the Marshals' office. All it took was some

sweet-talking, some wine and a few dinners to convince her she was in love with the creep. She managed to find out where you'd been placed and passed the information to him, but nothing else. She didn't have access to begin with so she shouldn't have even been able to learn that much."

"Wow," said Cory. "The things people do for love."

"Or when they think it's love. Anyway, she's been arrested, and procedures are going to be changed, or so I've been promised, although that's not going to be a problem for you anymore."

Cory smiled at him. "No, I guess it isn't."

Gage smiled back. "You'll still have to make a sworn statement for the FBI, and identify Ordano as the man who killed your husband. And there are going to be some other charges related to what happened last night. But one thing for absolute certain, you are never going to have to worry about that man again."

She couldn't stop smiling. "It's a wonderful feeling. I can't tell you how wonderful."

"I think I can imagine." Then Gage looked at Wade. "We've got a place for you as a deputy if you decide you want to hang around. Just think about it."

Rising, he picked up his hat and nodded to them both. "I'll call when we need your statement. It'll probably be later today or early tomorrow."

"I'm free." Free. At last. And how good it felt.

When Gage left, however, other thoughts tried to crowd in. Feeling suddenly nervous, and not sure she even wanted to hear the answer, but needing to know how many possibilities might lie before her, she said to Wade, "Will you take the job with the sheriff?"

"I don't know. I'll think about it. I guess it depends."

Her heart slammed uncomfortably. "Depends on what?"

Wade turned toward her, looking suddenly remote. Or was it something else she saw in his dark eyes. Concern? Unease? She couldn't quite read him.

"On whether you want me to hang around."

She caught her breath and her mouth went dry. Speech seemed impossible. But as she remained silent, she saw his face start to harden into stone again, and near panic struck her. She couldn't let him do that. No matter how hard it was for her to make herself utterly vulnerable to the wound he could inflict on her heart.

"I want you to hang around," she said almost breathlessly.

At once his face began to thaw. "Do you mean that?"

She took her newfound courage in her hands. "I mean I never want you to leave."

"Ever? You hardly know me."

"I know you well enough to know I don't want to give you up. Maybe you don't believe in love at first sight. I'm not sure I used to. It took me a while to fall in love with Jim. But with you…" She hesitated. "Wade, I've been in love before. I know what it is. All of it, good and bad. And I know for certain that I am in love with you."

For a moment he remained perfectly still. Her heart began to beat a nervous tattoo, for fear she had tried to claim something he wasn't prepared to let anyone claim. After all, he'd said he couldn't make connections.

"I think…I think I'm in love with you, too," he said. "I never felt this way before, so I'm not sure of anything except…I always want to be with you. Nobody's ever made me feel what you make me feel. I never knew a hug could mean so much or feel so good. I never knew I could get so intensely preoccupied with another person that I hang on to every word, every look, every gesture. I want to make you happy, if you'll just show me how. I want never to hurt you. Is that love?"

She leaned toward him and wrapped her arms around him. A moment later his closed around hers. "I want this forever," she whispered.

"Me, too." A sigh escaped him. "I want to marry you. I want to know that you want to marry me. For the first time in my life, Cory, I want the ring and the promises. Do you?"

She tilted her head up and looked at him, hoping her heart was in her eyes. "I want them, too, Wade, and I thought I'd never want them again. But I want them with you."

"So will you marry me?"

She watched the sun dawn on his face as she answered, simply, "Yes."

Then he pulled her onto his lap and kissed her, making this deepest of connections in the best way he knew how.

And with that kiss, they ushered in the dawn.

\* \* \* \* \*

# COMING NEXT MONTH

## Available December 28, 2010

ROMANTIC SUSPENSE

# REQUEST YOUR FREE BOOKS!

## 2 FREE NOVELS
## PLUS
## 2 FREE GIFTS!

ROMANTIC
SUSPENSE

*Sparked by Danger, Fueled by Passion.*

SRS10R

# HARLEQUIN®

## A Romance

### FOR EVERY MOOD™

Spotlight on

## Classic

Quintessential, modern love stories
that are romance at its finest.

See the next page
to enjoy a sneak peek from
the Harlequin Presents® series.

*Harlequin Presents® is thrilled
to introduce the first installment of
an epic tale of passion and drama by*
**USA TODAY** *Bestselling Author*
*Penny Jordan!*

*When buttoned-up Giselle first meets
the devastatingly handsome Saul Parenti,
the heat between them is explosive....*

"LET ME GET THIS STRAIGHT. Are you actually suggesting that I would stoop to that kind of game playing?"

Saul came out from behind his desk and walked toward her. Giselle could smell his hot male scent and it was making her dizzy, igniting a low, dull, pulsing ache that was taking over her whole body.

Giselle defended her suspicions. "You don't want me here."

"No," Saul agreed, "I don't."

And then he did what he had sworn he would not do, cursing himself beneath his breath as he reached for her, pulling her fiercely into his arms and kissing her with all the pent-up fury she had aroused in him from the moment he had first seen her.

Giselle certainly *wanted* to resist him. But the hand she raised to push him away developed a will of its own and was sliding along his bare arm beneath the sleeve of his shirt, and the body that should have been arching away from him was instead melting into him.

Beneath the pressure of his kiss he could feel and taste her gasp of undeniable response to him. He wanted to devour her, take her and drive them both until they were equally satiated—even whilst the anger within him that she should make him feel that way roared and burned its resentment of his need.

She was helpless, Giselle recognized, totally unable to withstand the storm lashing at her, able only to cling to the man who was the cause of it and pray that she would survive.

Somewhere else in the building a door banged. The sound exploded into the sensual tension that had enclosed them, driving them apart. Saul's chest was rising and falling as he fought for control; Giselle's whole body was trembling.

Without a word she turned and ran.

*Find out what happens when Saul and Giselle succumb to their irresistible desire in*

### THE RELUCTANT SURRENDER

*Available January 2011 from Harlequin Presents®*

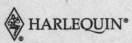